About The Author

Father Brian D'Arcy was born in Co. Fermanagh in June 1945 and is one of a family of four, two boys and two girls. He was educated at Mullymesker Primary School and Omagh CBS before going to St Michael's College, Enniskillen, to complete his secondary education.

He entered the Passionist Religious Congregation in 1962 and was professed at The Graan, Enniskillen, in 1963. He began his university education at UCD in 1963 and pursued his studies for the priesthood in Mount Argus Monastery, Dublin, (1963 – 67) and in Cloonamahon, Co. Sligo (1968-70). He was ordained a Passionist priest in 1969 in St Michael's College, Enniskillen.

In August 1970 he was appointed editor of The Cross *magazine and resided in Mount Argus until 1975, when he was appointed production editor of the Catholic Communications Centre in Dublin. Later he served for many years as parish priest at Mount Argus in Dublin, before returning to Enniskillen in 1989 as Superior of St. Gabriel's Retreat, The Graan. He left to become Superior in Crossgar but returned as Superior of The Graan in January 2001.*

His career in journalism began in 1966 when he wrote regularly for various pop magazines at home and abroad. He was the first priest in Ireland to be admitted to the National Union of Journalists. His weekly column in the Sunday World *has been running for 30 years. Brian D'Arcy is a well-known broadcaster and television personality. He had his own talk show on BBC Ulster ('Be My Guest') and hosted 'Straight Talking' with Brian D'Arcy for BBC TV. He is a 'Pause For Thought' contributor on Terry Wogan's morning show on BBC Radio 2. He now broadcasts a weekly programme with BBC Radio Ulster, 'Sunday With Brian D'Arcy'. He has broadcast for 2 FM and RTE Radio 1 for decades.*

He is a self-confessed 'fanatical' sports enthusiast. Among his more unusual pastimes is his voluntary role as chaplain to the entertainment industry. This brings him into close contact with the major personalities in showbusiness.

Through his ministry Fr Brian has worked in different parts of Ireland as well as the USA. He spent two terms in South Africa and he regards this as the most fruitful period of his life. His favourite charity is the Helping Hand Fund, which helps the poor of Ireland, north and south. All profits from this book will go to the Helping Hand Fund.

A Little Bit
of
LIFE

Father Brian D'Arcy

ISBN: 1 873223 14 5

First Published September 2005

Acknowledgement

The author and publishers are grateful to the Sunday World for permission to reprint these pieces. Sources of quotations are indicated in the text. In some cases it has not been possible to trace original sources: the authors of any such extracts should contact the publishers to ensure acknowledgement in future editions.

Typeset by Vision16, Galway
Printed and bound in Ireland by Leinster Leader

Cover photograph courtesy of Michael Ruddy ss.cc.

Published at Boa Vista, 31 The Baily, Galway

Contents

Introduction

It is often said that doubt is the opposite of faith. It isn't. The opposite of faith is certainty. This book is for the doubters. It's about faith, hope, love, life, healing and compassion. It's about misery and mercy. Life has taught me that where misery and mercy meet, you find compassion. Compassion shows itself in healing and in happiness.

If you're at a point in life where you're not sure about anything anymore, you'll find consolation within these pages. It is written especially for you.

The book deals with real problems from real life. Many of the stories come from my thirty years writing for the *Sunday World*. The readers have trusted me enough to share their life stories with me. I now share them with you, not to judge, but to learn from them. Thank you for your honesty and your generosity.

You'll find more questions than answers but, as Kris Kristofferson once said, 'Life is the question and life is the answer; God is the reason and love is the way.'

If there's one theme which sums up the book, it is this: Don't judge yourself too harshly. If you're still searching, then you're still on the journey and you're in a good place. That's life! Doubt is not the opposite of faith, certainty is.

I have tried to carry through the practical, no-nonsense approach of my column in this collection. At times it may seem over-critical of the Church as an institition. That is not my intention. I have given my entire life to the Church and even though I'm sometimes uncomfortable with what we've done in the past, and what we still do to people, it is and always will be my home.

The aim of this book is to help you realise that you too have a home in God's Kingdom. We don't have to be perfect, we don't have to to live up to every ideal, we don't have to know all the answers. All God asks is that we appreciate the gifts He has given us and that we use them for the good of His people. We learn more compassion than perfection from God (Mt. 5.48) .

Despite our doubts, or maybe because of them, God is all around us. As one of the reflections in the book points out, 'If you can look at the sunset and smile, if you can find beauty in the colour of a small flower, if you can find pleasure in the movement of a butterfly, if the smile of a child can still warm your heart, if you can see the good in other people, if the rain breaking on a rooftop call lull you to sleep, and if the sight of a rainbow makes you stop and stare in wonder, then you still have hope.'

As you go through the pages of the book, I hope you will be consoled and encouraged that there are others who share your burdens, your problems, your hopes and your aspirations. You are not alone in your search and your life has meaning.

As always, the best way to read this book is in small bites, well digested. Don't read it at one sitting. Dip in and out when it suits you. God will send you the inspiration you need.

As you journey through the pages you'll learn about your own goodness, feel at home in an imperfect Church, learn to accept who you are, and discover new ways to pray. You'll be challenged by people sharing their stories of abuse, cancer, addiction and AIDS. If you're an outcast and think your life's a failure because you're gay, you'll find many words of encouragement and none of condemnation. You'll be healed by laughter and hugged by the handicapped. Most of all, you'll be at peace with your own humanity.

Father Brian D'Arcy

The Graan
Enniskillen
Co. Fermanagh

Love and Doggedness

Not long ago two young men and their girlfriends called unannounced to see me. They were on their way to a holiday in Donegal and spotted the sign for The Graan outside Enniskillen.

It clicked with them that they might find me in. They were lucky. I was. It doesn't happen often.

I didn't know who they were and I still don't know why they called. But once they got a cup of tea and a biscuit they loosened up considerably.

One of them asked a question which baffled me. And then demanded an immediate answer. It was this: 'Why do you stay a priest in a church that is collapsing all around you?'

As it happened I was feeling a certain sense of guilt that day. I belong to the generation of priests who started out in life being part of a church which was bursting at the seams with enthusiasm and hope. Thirty years later it has gone from boom to bust with no sign of a boom again during my lifetime. The guilt comes from being part of a church which blew it.

I look around the emptying churches and notice that many of the generations between the ages of 15 and 45 are invariably absent. Seminaries are empty.

There aren't any young priests these days. The few who do come through are old men long before their time. Many of them are good, but will exercise their goodness on their own terms only.

One of my young visitors chipped in: 'If you were to listen to the bishops you'd think the only way forward was backwards.' I wouldn't have put it like that but I couldn't argue with it either.

So why do I stay? Pretty much, I suspect, for the same reason as you do. A mixture of love and doggedness. But that isn't enough to keep the spirits alive so I tried to explain it as simply as I could.

I told them I believed we are on the way to a new church. I explained that when Christ rose from the dead after his Passion he wasn't just a dead Christ who had been resuscitated.

The risen Christ was new. Those who had lived with him before his death didn't even recognise him now. And anyone who had met him was profoundly changed by the experience. So not only was Christ new but the people he met became new people too.

I believe that is where the church is going. I don't know what shape it will take but it will be a new church. All the old dead wood of authoritarianism and clericalism, putting people down, control freaks and people who manipulate others by misusing their authority, will all disappear.

The only hope is for a church of the laity where all, especially women, will be allowed their say.

If our leaders only had the sense to see it, the church they are trying to prop up is already dead. And most of us, if we had sense, would pull the rug from under their feet rather than give them a zimmer frame to steady themselves.

Right now, I told my visitors, we are on the first steps of a crucifixion which we thoroughly deserve. But the crucifixion will give life. We will rise again, by the grace of God, to a completely new vision of community and church. I firmly believe that. I may not see it in my lifetime. But I already see the beginnings of change.

So questions like whose fault is it that the church is collapsing are not worth asking. When Jesus rose from the dead there were no recriminations. But he did leave the gift of peace and promised us the Holy Spirit. And you can't predict where the Spirit will lead us.

Today we are hung up on using Mass attendance as the sole criterion for a good or bad Catholic. It only recently struck me that the vast majority of human beings, whether they are Catholic or not, will never go to Mass. And if that shocks you so be it. Get ready for another shock – the vast majority of them will never go to the sacrament of reconciliation either.

It's time we realised that, when it comes to forgiveness, God's hands are not tied. If Mass and confession were the only means of being saved then Jesus would have died in vain. Deep down we all know these things but we have to first admit them to ourselves.

A Few Simple Steps Towards a Happier Life

They say a pessimist is an optimist who knows. Over the years at the Novena of Hope at The Graan in Enniskillen, I have listened to gifted speakers from all walks of life.

Mostly they told their own stories. This is what I picked up. It is a fact that nobody can feel positive about life all the time. So how we look at life is as important as what happens to us in life.

None of the speakers put it as bluntly as this, but I believe the following steps will go a long way to developing a positive outlook on life.

1. First of all leave the past behind.

We all burn energy making martyrs of ourselves. Worse still are the 'if only brigade'.

It's as simple as this. What has happened can't be undone. So don't make things worse by throwing a good life after a bad one. There's not a person on earth who doesn't wish that they had lived life differently.

Make up your mind to let things go. That way you give yourself permission to have a fresh start.

2. Don't make the same mistakes over and over again.

If something goes wrong think about it, spot where it went wrong, then take some action to ensure it doesn't go wrong next time.

If you have made a mess of things and said something stupid to another person, don't let it simmer. Say sorry, admit your mistake, it won't kill you. It's not the mistake which is the problem, but how we handle it.

3. Stop putting yourself down.

Demeaning yourself is not a virtue. It is an insult to yourself and to the God who made you. Being modest is perfectly acceptable. Being a groveller isn't. If somebody gives you a compliment say thanks and mark it off as a success.

4. Stop worrying about what others think of you.

If you make a mistake it proves one thing. You are part of the human race. But if you paralyse yourself by wondering what other people think, you could be surprised to discover they don't think about you at all. It's your life, make your own decisions.

5. Take charge of your life.

No-one will make things happen for you. You have to make things happen for yourself. And no matter what bad things happen to you in life, do your best to turn it around.

6. Knock down your ivory tower.

More and more people afraid of getting hurt build a tower around them selves. They trust no one.

If you keep people out, they will never hurt you, but you'll never live positively either.

7. Be grateful.

Those who are grateful for their gifts are always more positive than those who spend their lives complaining about gifts they don't have. Take time to think about what you have and be grateful for it.

8. Like yourself.

It seems obvious when you say it. If you don't like yourself why should anybody else like you?

There will be things about yourself that you don't like. Then change them. Don't use them as an excuse to hate yourself. I have always found it useful to list five gifts and then try to prioritise them.

Make the most of your opportunities and never stop working on yourself to be better.

That's what I have learned at the Novena of Hope. I also learned that a promise can never take the place of a performance, so now that I have got a handle on it, it's time to put it into practice. Maybe that's the most hopeful thing of all.

Sneaking Good People Into Heaven

As I fast approach the latter years of life, more and more publishers try to persuade me to write an autobiography.

So far I've refused, despite serious pressure. But if I ever give in, one of the chapters will be: HOW TO SNEAK GOOD PEOPLE INTO HEAVEN.

I'll write about God's mercy, God's love, God's promises and how the power freaks who have taken over churches give Him a bad name. They waste their lives inventing sins to send people to hell, while God fills heaven despite their best efforts. They live in a world known only to themselves (thankfully), they kill God's spirit. Every time we find something which attracts people to a relationshipwith God, they find ways to forbid it and condemn it.

The long list of bishops making futile statements condemning penitential services which people find meaningful is embarrassing. I don't know who they think they're kidding. Lay people have them sussed. It has little to do with theology, nothing to do with spirituality and everything to do with abuse of their power. Anyone who prays the Gospels realises how Jesus Himself treated sinners.

Every day I read the Gospels I marvel how often Jesus tells us no one should put limits to God's kingdom, let alone exclude people from it. People who try to do the right thing and genuinely seek peace with God, have a place in God's kingdom which no priest, no bishop, no clerical civil servant in Rome, no Pope even, can take from them.

The sad thing is that these men – and they are all men who are even older than I am – make religion and the Church they claim to represent, irrelevant. To talk about cross-dressing as always being a mortal sin, for example, becomes ridiculous when we clerics are seen as cross-dressers every time we go on an altar. Do they not realise what people think and say?

We need to encourage a mature attitude to sin and life. I'm in the fortunate position that I still spend hours every week with people trying to find their peace. It's always discouraging when penitents ramble through a list of sins which mean nothing to God or anyone else.

It's so rewarding though, when young and old come into the room, sit down and chat about where they are in life. They usually have a dreadful sense of their own worth and, if anything, judge themselves too harshly. My task is to help them find their gifts, their talents, and their goodness and to be grateful for the grace they have received. From there they can see more clearly where they are failing and where they can improve.

More important still is to recognise that confessing as such is not the central part of the sacrament or the process. God's mercy is. Lists come from the era of the God of fear. It puts the emphasis in the wrong place.

God is the centre of the spiritual life. Responsibility and gratitude grow out of a recognition that we owe everything to the God of love. If you really want to know what God is like, you'll find the truth in the Gospels. Two Gospel stories stand out. In the story of the Prodigal Son, the sinner (son) prepared his list well, but God (the father) didn't want to know. He was looking out for his return, saw it was genuine, wrapped his arms around him, forgave him and ordered a party to celebrate. That's the truth.

Again, when the first pope sinned by denying Jesus, he was treated with respect. Jesus didn't force him or the other failed disciples to crawl. He asked one question only: 'Do You Love Me?' In the end, it's all that matters.

Be Positive!

I was amazed recently to find the following six pieces of advice given to retired people. It was supposed to make them feel better. To help them cope with the feeling of being passed over. Would they help you?

1. Stop feeling sorry for yourself.
2. Seek out good things to do.
3. Keep your mind and your muscles occupied. Read and take exercises.
4. Have a good sense of humour.
5. Stop complaining and start being thankful.
6. Give of yourself in any way you can

It set me thinking of the various excuses we use as little emotional road blocks on our way through life.

If any of the following 10 excuses are familiar and recognisable, let me give you a few tips on how to get round the road blocks.

1. I can't take it anymore.

After a day listening to other peoples' troubles I quite regularly come to the conclusion that I can't take any more. Yet Socrates offered good advice.

He said: 'If all our misfortunes were laid in one pile from which everyone had to take an equal portion, most people would be content to take back their own and depart.'

If we think our own problems are bad, ask yourself would you want to take on someone else's crosses. Learn to live with some problems and ask for strength to cope with those we can do nothing about.

2. My life is so empty.

I admit it's true. Our lives are empty. We have good friends, good ideas and achievements to be proud of in our life. The real trick is being able to recognise them.

An empty life is best coped with by trying to see the good we can do for others, the good we may have achieved, and the good that we may still achieve little by little.

3. Nothing I do makes the slightest difference.

Actually nothing could be further from the truth.

Almost all great achievements in human history have been accomplished because one person had the guts and the courage to do it.

4. I haven't got what it takes.

You may not have what it takes to rule the world but you have what it takes to do what you can do best.

No matter what our limitations are, each of us can do something to ease the burden of other people.

You have got what it takes if you set yourself realistic goals.

5. If I could only get away from it all.

Let's put it straight. We all need rest. And we do need to get away from it all occasionally. But the temptation constantly to run away from it is one of the reasons why we have so many addicted people. It is probably the single most important reason why we have the kind of society we have.

6. Nobody cares about me.

You are probably half right. But then do you care about anybody either?

When I get the feeling that nobody cares about me, I usually conclude that people do care about me but don't show it in the way I'd like them to. I have met people for whom it could be truly said that nobody cares. But not often. If we make ourselves vulnerable there are always people who care.

7. I just can't keep up with everything.

Who can? You have to be selective. Even if you can't keep up with everything it doesn't mean you're a failure. Only God can keep up with everything. Our task is to select what we can keep up with, leave the rest aside and accept that we are normal human beings.

8. What's the use of trying?

God doesn't ask us to be a success but he did ask us to try. We might not be able to foresee how the projects we begin will end, but unless we try we can certainly predict how it will end. In failure.

9. You can't beat the system.

Sometimes it's a good thing that we 'can't beat the system,' because the system might very well be right. It is also comforting to know that almost any system can be beaten.

10. People are no bloody good.

Here's a little parable for you. A teacher was taking over a class for the first time. She looked at the roll book and saw the IQs marked off for each child.

They were 138, 140, 141, etc. She was delighted to know she had such a bright and wonderful class.

So she began to try new methods with the students and they responded well to her creative approach.

It was only later she found out that the figures after each pupil's name stood not for their IQ but for their locker numbers.

The moral of the story is that most of the time people will be as positive or negative as we expect them to be.

The Special Child

The Child, yet unborn, spoke with the Father,
'Lord, how will I survive in the world?
I will not be like other children, My
Walk may be slower, my speech hard
To understand, I may look different.
What is to become of me?'
The Lord replied to the child,
'My precious one, have no fear, I will
give you exceptional Parents, they
will love you because you are special,
not in spite of it. Though your path
through life will be difficult, your
reward will be greater, you will have been blessed
with a special ability to love,
and those whose lives you touch will be blessed
because you are special.'

(Author unknown)

Are you Ready to Have Kids?
Try these Simple Tests!

Toy Test

Open the largest available box of lego. Have a friend spread the bits all over the house. Put on a blindfold and take off shoes. Try to walk to the bathroom or kitchen. Do not scream as this would waken a child at night.

Grocery Store Test

Borrow one or two small animals (goats are best) and take them with you as you shop. Always keep them in sight and pay for anything they eat or damage.

Dressing Test

Obtain one large, unhappy live octopus. Stuff it into a small net bag making sure that all the arms stay inside.

Feeding Test

Obtain a large plastic milk jug. Fill halfway with water. Suspend from the ceiling with a cord. Start the jug swinging. Try to insert spoonfuls of soggy cereal into the mouth of the jug while pretending to be an aeroplane. Now dump the contents of the jug on the floor.

Night Test

Prepare by obtaining a small cloth bag and fill it with 8-12 pounds of sand. Soak it thoroughly in water. At 3.00pm begin to waltz and hum with the bag until 9.00pm. Lay down your bag and set your alarm for 10.00pm. Get up, pick up your bag and sing every song you have ever heard. Make up about a dozen more and sing these too until 4.00am. Set alarm for 5.00am. Get up and make breakfast. Keep this up for five years. Look cheerful.

Car Test
Forget the Jaguar and buy a station wagon. Buy a chocolate ice cream cone and put it in the glove compartment and leave it there. Get a two cent piece and stick it into the CD player. Take a family size package of chocolate chip cookies and mash them into the back seat. Run a rake across both sides of the car.

Physical Test (Woman)
Obtain a large bean bag and attach it to the front of your clothes. Leave it there for 9 months. Then remove the beans. And try not to notice your wardrobe full of clothes. You won't be wearing them for a while.

Physical Test (Men)
Go to the nearest pharmacy. Set your wallet on the counter. Ask the assistant to help himself. Now proceed to the nearest supermarket. Go to the head office and arrange for your salary to be directly paid to the supermarket. Purchase a newspaper. Go home and read it quietly for the last time.

Final Assignment
Find a couple who already have a small child. Lecture them on how they can improve their discipline, patience, tolerance, toilet training and child's table manners. Suggest many ways that they can improve. Emphasize to them that they should never allow their children to run wild. Enjoy this experience. It will be the last time that you have all the answers.

The Signs of Inner Peace

We need to be on the look out for symptoms of inner peace... It is possible that people everywhere could come down with it in epidemic proportions.

This could pose a serious threat to the condition known as *conflict* in the world. Here are some signs and symptoms of inner peace which should alarm you:

- a tendency to think and act spontaneously rather than on fears based on past experience
- an unmistakable ability to enjoy each moment
- loss of interest in being judgmental of other people
- loss of interest in conflict of all kinds
- loss of ability to worry – in itself a serious symptom of inner peace
- frequent overwhelming episodes of appreciation
- contented feelings of connectedness with others and with nature
- frequent attacks of smiling and even laughter
- an increased tendency to let things happen rather than the urge to make them happen

If you have two or more of these symptoms, you are in grave danger of being out of step with the rest of the world.

Letter of Love

'Not so long ago, through my parish bulletin, I invited divorced and remarried people to come to the Eucharist in my church.'

That was a startling opening to a letter I got from a priest in England, who wishes to remain anonymous.

He was writing in response to some of the things I said recently, pleading with church authorities to show more interest in people than in law. To deal with people individually, not as a herd.

'I read the article in the *Sunday World* and I could share your frustration. When I invited the divorced and remarried to receive communion, it had a wonderful effect on our parish community.

'People who were alienated became part of the Body of Christ again. It was the most effective thing I've ever done in 30 years of priestly work,' the priest recalled.

'Unfortunately I couldn't do it now. The church that we all loved and gave our lives to, is being destroyed by legalists who know nothing of Christ's burning desire to help people through difficult times.

'These are some of the things I wrote which helped so many people.

'I know the Church says that you aren't free to receive the Eucharist if you remarry without first receiving an annulment. But there are many other truths the Church holds dear. Truths that justify my inviting you to Communion. And there are many truths that the Church has yet to learn. Truths that you may already grasp intuitively.

'Any time love dies and for whatever reason, it's a tragedy. Divorce can destroy everyone involved. No victim is ever the same again; children and the extended family and friends are all marked by the pain of separation. Its consequences can be devastating and long-lasting.

'The Church, rightly, has high ideals about your marriage. Couples must enter it with maturity, freedom and knowledge. They must be capable of establishing a lifelong faithful relationship that is open to children. If a marriage ends, the Church is willing to examine it to see if it was indeed a true marriage in the full sense of the word. If they decide that some of the essential elements were lacking, you'll be given an annulment and you then can marry in Church because, according to the Church, you've never been married in the first place.

'The problem is that sometimes the annulment process is unnecessarily complicated and drawn out. You may have been discouraged from filing an annulment by priests who don't understand the process. And even if you do go through the process your chances of being granted an annulment are extremely thin.

'So I want you to realise that there are many reasons why you married without receiving an annulment and while I don't know your reasons personally, I assume that you acted in good faith at all times.

'My next point is not so easy to grasp but is even more important. Receiving Communion has nothing to do with justifying a good life. But it has everything to do with a need to lead a good life. It used to be that if you led a good life then you could receive Communion worthily. Now we realise that no one is worthy to receive Communion anyway.

'Furthermore, Christ came to call not the righteous, but sinners and in the Eucharist he feeds those who hunger for mercy.

'So staying away from the Eucharist when you're struggling honestly to pick up the pieces is like staying away from the doctor when you're sick. Eucharist is the medicine that helps you.

'Nobody deserves the Eucharist. You can't earn it nor can you demand it. You do need to change. You need to mend your relationships, let go of bitterness and fear and forgive those who have wounded you and seek forgiveness from those you have hurt. You need to fulfil the obligations of your previous marriage, especially to your children.

'It seems to me it's impossible to do those things without the grace of the Eucharist in your life. So I invite you then to come to the Eucharist because Communion isn't a sign of God's approval, but rather a sign of God's acceptance of your struggle.'

It's at time like this you realise that good people haven't rejected the Church. On the contrary. Lawyers and legalists have hijacked the Church, and Christ's compassion for sinners struggling with their lives rarely gets a look in.

When Love Dies

'I am writing to you out of sheer desperation. I am in the process of getting a legal separation.

'I have been married for over 20 years with some of the most beautiful children on this planet.

'We have spoken of separation many times and always said it would not be possible so as not to hurt the family any more.

'But the past two years have been a nightmare for me. One horror after another.'

That's how Aileen (not her real name) sees her life so far. It's a sad letter that brilliantly sums up what can go wrong. Be sure to read her ten reasons for leaving and I defy you not to have compassion.

'I was 18 when I got married and had a 10-month-old baby. At the time it wasn't a problem. The church and the priest were very helpful. Now that I'm trying to get a separation I have to go through the District Court and The Circuit Court.

'I have to pay solicitors and barristers and be at the mercy of a judge as I recall the most intimate and horrible details of what happened within my home.

'I need proof from the gardai, the medical profession, and have witnesses to back up my statements.

'I have to tell them about physical violence and, worse still, mental violence.

'People encouraged me to do it and say that I will be better off with him out of my life. But they forget that the last thing I ever wanted to do was to break up the family unit.

'The family is the most sacred unit in the world. Everything should be done to keep it intact.

'As I have tried to come to terms with the loss of my marriage, and regain my confidence, self esteem and my place in the world, I have written down ten reasons to justify my separation.

'I wish I could say all this to my family, friends and neighbours but at the moment I'm being avoided like the plague. No one wants to take sides. Maybe you will explain sometime the difference between taking sides and giving support:

1. I did not deserve to be verbally abused.
2. I did not deserve to go through mental torture by being threatened with suicide by a person I once loved.
3. I did not deserve to have to watch while knives were sharpened in preparation for suicide, nor did I deserve to watch while a bullet was loaded into a humane killer for the same purpose.
4. I did not deserve to have to go to bed to make love to the person who did these things to me.
5. I did not deserve to be pushed out of my room and thrown out of my home.
6. I did not deserve to be told in front of my children that I was a terrible mother and to pray that they would never meet anyone like me because I was evil, deceitful and a liar.
7. I did not deserve to be pulled around the room naked from the waist up because I wasn't heard saying good night.
8. I did not deserve to have to call my son to help me escape through a window in the middle of the night and travel in my night attire for 10 miles for safety.
9. I did not deserve to be terrorised by drunks sent to my home threatening me.
10. I did not deserve years of being pulled down, held up to ridicule, constantly watched, followed and every move I made to be written down and held against me in court simply because I wanted a separation.

'Thanks for listening.'

No, dear lady. Thank you for writing.

We Need More About Love And Less About Sex

Pornography is rightly in the news these days. There is no doubt that pornography is harmful. It damages those who create it and those who use it.

It diminishes human dignity and mutilates all of us, sometimes more than we recognise. When it victimises children it is at its most horrific.

Pornography has been around a long time. They say it was scratched on the walls of caves.

Pornography needs to be put in context. It is the result of another problem. Our troubles begin when the sense of the sacred is taken out of sex.

Too often, what passes for Church teaching falls into the same trap as pornography. It talks about sex in an abstract and wholly inhuman way. Like pornography, it strips sex of the sacred.

It's part of a modern malaise. Listen to people talking. Have you noticed that nobody falls in love anymore? They have 'a relationship.' Hardly anyone 'makes love.' But they are obsessed with 'having sex.'

Courtship is a dirty word. And for many, marriage is no longer a truly romantic adventure. It's more like a court room battle over contracts and commitments, territory and power.

Talk shows seem to thrive on imprudent people being willing to blab like idiots about intimate details of their love life.

Sex with no sense of the sacred means that 'anything goes, because nothing matters.'

And so sex is seen as mechanistic, amoral, easy, inhuman – without love and without dignity. We need more about love and less about sex.

What, for example, does the Church say these days to single people? If you were to put all the statements about sex and the single Catholic in a book it would be a slim volume.

A woman I spoke with had been married for 19 years to a man who abused her because of his addiction to alcohol.

When she married she was a conservative 21 year-old petrified virgin.

Everything was clear. She didn't have to make any decisions.

Now that the marriage is long gone, she faces a new set of decisions. As a result it took her three years before she felt comfortable enough to date someone else.

And when you hear a 45 year-old woman with a lot of experience say: 'I don't think God is all that concerned about responsible adults fulfilling their sexual needs,' you listen carefully and make suggestions tentatively.

She is totally against indiscriminate sex but sees it differently for mature adults who have reached a mutual decision after a lot of searching.

One of her friends who is slightly older and in a similar position had an even stronger view.

'I don't think I need to beg God's forgiveness for making love,' she said.

'I don't carry around a lot of guilt regarding sexual experiences I have had because I believe it to be a responsible decision.'

The basis of her view is that sex between two caring adults is an expression of love. It's an integral part of a sharing, loving relationship.

So how's the Church going to make them feel at home?

If you want a grown-up Church you have to start treating people like grown-ups and stop treating them like juveniles.

The Church has the right and the duty to teach clearly and compassionately about sex, sexuality, marriage and morality in general.

But these days people will come to their own responsible conclusions about the use of their sexuality. So what is said better be real and reasonable.

And God Created Mothers

When the good Lord was creating mothers, He was into his sixth day of overtime. An angel appeared and said, 'You're doing a lot of fiddling around on this one.'

And the Lord said, 'Have you read the specifications on this order? She has to be completely washable but not plastic….. run on black coffee and left-overs… have a lap that disappears when she stands up… a kiss that can cure anything from a broken leg to a disappointed love affair… and six pairs of hands.'

The angel shook her head slowly and said, 'Six pairs of hands? No way.'

'It's not the hands that are causing the problems,' said the Lord, 'it's the three pairs of eyes that mothers have to have. One pair that sees through closed doors when she asks, "What are you children doing in there?" when she already knows. Another in the back of her head that sees what she shouldn't but what she has to know. And, of course, the ones in front that can look at a child when he gets himself into trouble and say I understand and I love 'you' without so much as uttering a word."

'Lord' said the angel, touching his sleeve gently, 'go to bed, Tomorrow is another..'

'I can't,' said the Lord. 'I'm so close now. Already I have one who heals herself when she is sick, can feed a family of six on one pound of mince, and can get a nine-year-old to have a bath.' The angel circled the model of a mother very slowly. 'It's too soft,' the angel sighed. 'But tough!' said the Lord excitedly. 'You cannot imagine what this mother can endure.'

'Can it think?'

'Not only think, but it can reason and compromise,' said the Creator. Finally, the angel bent over and ran her finger across the cheek. 'There's a leak,' she pronounced.

'It's not a leak,' said the Lord, 'it's a tear.'

'What's it for?' asked the angel.

'It's for joy, sadness, disappointment, pain, loneliness and pride.'

'You are a genius!' said the angel.

The Lord looked sombre. 'I didn't put it there.'

And They Lived Happily Ever After…

I was looking at my diary for the coming year and I'm delighted there are so many weddings in it.

I love assisting at marriages. They fill me with hope. Celebrating love is marvellous. Here are a few wedding stories that always give me a laugh.

A young bride-to-be learned to her dismay that some of her future husband's religious beliefs didn't comply with her own. 'What should I do?' she asked her mother anxiously. 'He doesn't even believe in Hell.'

'Don't worry dear,' her mother replied, 'Between the two of us we'll show him how wrong he is.'

When the morning of the marriage came the bride-to-be was very nervous. The thought of walking the long aisle up the church made her panic. The mother then tried to calm her. 'Don't worry, dear,' her mother said, 'you can get rid of your jitters if you concentrate on three words.

'First, think of the *aisle*. It's the same aisle you're walking down every Sunday since you were a little girl.

'Second, look up at the *altar* and just focus on it. When you focus on it, the length of the aisle will disappear. You'll find yourself getting nearer the altar with every step.

'Third, think about the *hymn*. Listen to the music. Think about the words. You have chosen it specially for this day and you'll get lost in the music.'

It worked like a charm. She kept repeating the three words to herself, 'Aisle…Altar…Hymn.' When she arrived on her groom's arm she was still repeating the words, 'Aisle…Altar…Hymn.' He got frightened because he knew then what the story of their marriage would be: *I'll alter him.*

When Mr. and Mrs Henry Ford celebrated their Golden Wedding Anniversary a reporter asked them, 'To what do you attribute your 50 years of successful married life?'

'The formula,' said Ford, 'is the same formula I have always used in making cars. Just stick to one model.'

Perhaps you have read *Looking Out for Number One*. But did you know that, after the book was published, the author's wife divorced him and is now receiving a fortune in alimony. When asked about this, she is reported to have said, 'I read the book.'

Why Worry?

Perhaps the best attitude of all is the 'Why Worry' riddle followed, they say, by the more irresponsible of us Irishmen. It goes something like this.

There are only two things to worry about: whether you are well or whether you are sick.

If you're well, there's nothing to worry about.
If you're sick, there are only two things to worry about: whether you'll get better or whether you'll die.

If you get better, you have nothing to worry about.
And if you're going to die, you have only two things to worry about: whether you go to Heaven or whether you go to Hell.

If you go to Heaven, you have nothing to worry about.

And if you go to Hell, you'll meet so many of your friends there, you'll feel very much at home, so why worry?

Laughter Is The Best Medicine

I always knew laughter was the best medicine. Now scientists have discovered that the old wives tale is in fact true.

There is a link between laughter and the ability to fight disease.

Research conducted at Indiana State University has prompted health professionals to look more seriously at humour as a complementary therapy.

In the study a group of women were asked to choose between a comedy video or a video on tourism. The people who watched Bill Cosby, Woody Allen and Robin Williams boosted their immune system much more effectively than those who watched tourism videos.

They found that the women who watched the comedy videos and laughed out loudly resisted all kinds of viruses as a result. In America Humour Workshops are already marketed as a help to self-healing. The researchers say that in general we laugh too little.

Laughter definitely is the best medicine. It is a universal language. It has been shown that adults laugh 20 times a day while children laugh more than 200 times a day.

Martin Luther in the 16th century said, 'If we are not allowed to laugh in heaven, I don't want to go there.' Yet, he himself was a manic-depressive. His wife had to tell him to brighten up. 'No wonder nobody believes in God when they look at your face,' she chided.

Humour is a strange thing. Would you find this story humorous for example?

After Mass the Pastor pulled Jack aside.

'You need to join the army of the Lord,' the pastor said.

'I'm already in the army of the Lord,' Jack replied.

'Then how come I see you only at Christmas and Easter?'

Jack lowered his voice to a whisper, 'I'm in the Secret Service.'

Last year a psychologist at the University of Hertfordshire launched a year long project to find the world's funniest joke. More than 10,000 jokes were submitted and 100,000 people in 70 countries voted for their favourite. The winning joke goes like this:

Two hunters are out in the woods when one falls to the ground. He doesn't seem to be breathing; his eyes are rolled back in his head.

The other guy gets on his mobile and calls the Emergency Services.

'My friend is dead,' he gasped to the operator. 'What can I do?'

The operator in a calm soothing voice says, 'Just take it easy. I can help. First, let's be sure he's dead.'

There is a silence and the hunter takes out his gun and shoots his friend in the head.

'Ok,' says the hunter back on the phone, 'Now what?'

Did you find that funny? Ok, then one more.

If college students had written the Bible:

- There would be only five Commandments.
- There would be a new interpretation of Biblical events – 'Why did Cain kill Abel?' Because they were roommates.
- Instead of creating the world in six days and resting on the seventh, God would have put it off and crammed the whole lot into the night before the seventh day.

Bless Me, Father, For I Have Crashed

Henry Cooper is one of the most famous and best-loved English boxers of all time. Henry was raised in poverty in South London, but used boxing as a way to get to the top, flattened Muhammad Ali when he was still Cassius Clay and was knighted some years ago.

He was the first boxer to receive a knighthood and, according to Henry, it was 'the cream on top of the cake. You get knights in other sports but I was the first one in boxing. So it wasn't just for me, it was for boxing too. I'm sorry me old Mum and Dad weren't alive to know that their South London boy had done good.'

Thirty years ago I did an interview in Henry's home. It was just after he retired and I found him to be a perfect gentleman. He brought me to meet his wife Albina who treated me royally. He gave the interview and all he asked in return was that I would bless his brand new Mercedes parked outside his front door. I gave it a thorough blessing, which delighted Henry and Albina. He left me back to the tube station and I flew back to Dublin.

Next day Liam Nolan, who was a personal friend of Henry's and who had arranged the interview for me, phoned inquiring how Henry was. Henry, I assured him was in the best of good health.

Liam was delighted to hear it and wondered how he had escaped injury in the car crash.

'What car crash?' I asked.

'Yesterday evening he crashed his new Mercedes car and it was a write-off according to the *Daily Mirro*r today,' Liam assured me. It was the first I heard of it.

I wrote a note of sympathy to Henry, wondering how I got my blessings mixed up. He sent me back a letter saying that there was no need to apologise. He and Albina agreed that had the car not been blessed he probably would have been killed.

Henry's faith was greater than mine. I take car blessings seriously ever since.

Christmas In Heaven

I see the countless Christmas trees around the world below
With tiny lights like Heaven's stars reflecting the snow.
The sight is so spectacular please wipe away the tear
For I'm spending Christmas with Jesus this year.

I hear the many Christmas songs that people hold so dear
But the sounds of music can't compare with the Christmas choir up here.
I have no words to tell you the joys their voices bring
For it's beyond description to hear the angels sing.

I know how much you miss me; I see the pain inside your heart
But I am not so far away, we really aren't apart.
So be happy for me, dear ones, you know I hold you dear
And be glad I'm spending Christmas with Jesus Christ this year.

I sent you each a special gift from my heavenly home above,
I sent you each a memory of my undying love.
After all love is a gift more precious than pure gold.
It was always most important in the stories Jesus told.

Please love and keep each other as my Father said to do.
For I can't count the blessing of love he has for each of you.
So have a merry Christmas and wipe away that tear.
Remember I am spending Christmas with Jesus Christ this year.

This lovely poem was written by a 13-year-old boy named Ben. He died of a brain tumour that he had battled with for over four years. He died on 14 December 1997. He gave this poem to his Mum before he died.

A Brave Young Voice

I'm always glad when young people read my newspaper column. I'm even more happy when they put pen to paper. This is what I mean.

'Over the past few weeks I have begun to read your column. It was your wonderful coverage on sex abuse and gays which make me read it every week now,' began the young lady, who is in her last year at Grammar School.

'I'm a girl of 17 and to be truthful I'm totally sick of hearing older people condemning young people.

'I presumed you'd be no different, since it was my mother who was always encouraging me to read you.

'I live in a good size town. The other night at Mass the priest got mad and we heard about sex before marriage and the evil of homosexuality. At the end I felt everything was a sin and I was very uncomfortable in the church. I felt I didn't belong there any more.

'He also said the media were ruining the Catholic Church because they blamed them for everything that's wrong in the country. He said this was unfair. I have to say I heartily agree with him. The media is unfair to Catholics.

'However there is one question I would like discussed. We all know that there are many people, young and old, who have sexual relationships outside marriage. There are many ways to avoid pregnancy. You can use condoms, the pill, etc. Yet the Catholic Church says that all of these are wrong.

'If you sleep with someone. If you get pregnant. If you use condoms it's all wrong. And if you have a termination of pregnancy that's the most serious crime of all – and I agree that abortion is evil. But what do you do?

'It's easy for older people who are married and clergy to criticise us. But there is a lot of pressure.

'I feel that I'm lucky that I have open parents. But even in our situation there is a limit to what I can ask.

'In school we have Biology but that's not the kind of question you'd ask there.

‘A few of my friends have slept with somebody, just to see what it was like. Does that mean they are bad?

‘Even on the subject of different religions, there seems to be some cover-up. I go to a school which has different religions in it but after spending almost all of second level education with Protestants I know very little about them.

‘In the town I come from there are two priests and one Protestant Minister. The younger priest, about 40, is very sarcastic and hurtful, the older priest is out-of-date but a nice man. And the Protestant Minister seems approachable.

‘The priests work hard and in times of trouble are very good to everybody.

‘Last Christmas we all went to confessions to keep our parents happy. But when I came out I felt I would never go back again. I told a few tiny sins, and I wanted to chat with the younger priest, but he gave me a lecture on what the Catholic Church says.

‘So that’s my predicament. Perhaps there are a few ideas which might give you food for thought.’

(Derry Teenager)

It was a letter which made me think. As the song says: ‘There are more questions than answers,’ but sometimes the questions point the way to loving answers. Think about it.

Stay in Touch With Your Young Ones

The woman at the concert the other night looked delightfully middle-aged as she linked her husband down the steps.

'You don't write much about teenagers any more,' she said without a word of introduction.

The truth is that I am not too confident I have any positive advice on how to handle today's teenagers.

Let me begin by saying my experience tells me they are absolutely brilliant. They have a lot of pressures. They have a range of choices that we couldn't dream of. They make mistakes the same as every generation did. But by and large they are absolutely brilliant.

They navigate their way through very stormy seas with great success.

In a way that is a compliment to parents too. Difficult as it is to be a teenager, it's an even more challenging time to be a parent.

It's a shock to watch the trusting child who chatted away happily grow into an argumentative, secretive and, sometimes, resentful teenager who challenges every thought and every principle a parent ever had.

It's also well to remember that parents of teenagers are usually going through a difficult time themselves. They are likely to be in the 40 to 50 age bracket, quite possibly plunging into a mid-life crisis.

Many parents are so taken up with their own life, their own worries, and their own relationship that they lose sight of the bigger picture and frankly have no great desire to listen to the worries of their teenage children who never had it so good.

Yet teenagers have mountains of problems. Fears about their future, anxiety about examination results, doubts about their own self-confidence and self-esteem, peer pressure, their changing appearance, drink, drugs, sexual feelings, the pressure to be sexually active and the need to be independent. It is any wonder life is a mess for them? When you are a teenager, the world can seem a cruel place.

If both parents and teenagers could share their worries, I suspect they would find they had more in common than they realised.

Communication, difficult as it can be, is a must.

If I had to sum up things on the back of an envelope these are some of the essentials I'd write down.

- Don't jump in. Think things out and you are less likely to regret what you say or do.
- Don't grow old too quickly. In other words, try to get into your teenager's world.
- Get to know your teenager because he or she is a different being from the child you used to know.
- Be fair to your teenager. Try to give him or her as much control and power as you can. Praise and encourage them.
- Talk things through even though it's driving you mad and you seem to lose every argument.
- Lastly, look after yourself. Parents are under stress and need their own time.

How to Stay Young

1. Throw out non-essential numbers. This includes age, weight and height. Let the doctors worry about them. That is why you pay them.
2. Keep only cheerful friends. The grouches pull you down.
3. Keep learning. Learn more about the computer, crafts, gardening, whatever. Never let the brain idle. 'An idle mind is the devil's workshop.' And the devil's name is Alzheimer's.
4. Enjoy the simple things.
5. Laugh often, long and loud. Laugh until you gasp for breath.
6. The tears happen. Endure, grieve, and move on. The only person who is with us our entire life, is ourselves. Be ALIVE while you are alive.
7. Surround yourself with what you love, whether it's family, pets, keepsakes, music, plants, hobbies, whatever. Your home is your refuge.
8. Cherish your health: If it is good, preserve it. If it is unstable, improve it. If it is beyond what you can improve, get help.
9. Don't take guilt trips. Take a trip to the mall, even to the next county, to a foreign country but NOT to where the guilt is.
10. Tell the people you love them, at every opportunity.

If Your Child Is Gay…

More and more parents come to me for advice on how to handle what to them is devastating news – their son or daughter is gay.

They come, usually, after a painful bewildering journey. It causes distress not only to the parents but, even more so, to the young person themselves. Most are at a loss as to how to respond.

Things are not helped by the attitudes of the churches. Recently both Anglicanism and Roman Catholicism have shown themselves to be confused, out of touch, and cruel in their approach to homosexuality.

They use language designed to hurt those struggling to come to terms with being gay. They are of no use to distressed parents trying to do the best they can, and who frequently blame themselves for the position about which the churches threaten them so dogmatically.

Invariably, those struggling with being gay, have a low self-esteem. This often transfers itself to the parents too.

Growing up in an environment where being gay is still stigmatised, makes it totally understandable. Imagine if you were mocked, bullied and isolated by your peers.

How would you feel? It's why so many build huge protective barriers around themselves. How would you like, in your formative years, hiding your true nature from your friends and classmates dreading that your 'secret' would ever get out?

I am convinced that is why so many gay adolescents have such a high incidence of attempted suicide.

The loneliness, the isolation they endure even in the best of families means they carry an unbearable burden of guilt and shame simply for being who and what they are. Self hatred is inevitable.

I don't pretend to have any answers for parents but perhaps a few questions might help.

You have to ask yourself what your first God - given task as a parent is. Surely the most important one is to help each of your children to be free, self sufficient, unique and totally themselves.

Most parents know that, whatever else, they want to accept their children as they are, affirm them and indeed celebrate their uniqueness.

Society and Churches make it extremely difficult to do so. Society and Churches are wrong.

Usually parents struggle to cope with their own perceived failures. It's as if some horrible scandal has happened to the family.

That doesn't help. Parents who talk about it, listen, read and most of all challenge their own convictions in the light of this new experience, usually do best.

It helps gay people if they can 'come out' to somebody. Usually 'coming out' to parents and families is the most crucial step of all. If that works, everything else will fall into place. If it doesn't, 'coming out' is seen as dangerous, risk-filled and leaving yourself open to rejection by those whom you want to love you most.

I believe that 'coming out' to a close group of people goes a long way towards self-acceptance and claiming one's true identity before God. It is a crucial moment.

Being in contact with other gay people and gay communities can be a great help to parents too. Their greatest worry is often that sexual behaviour can be both unhealthy and immoral.

It's important to give your child the freedom and the ability to take control of their own life and to determine their own future as an adult. It means listening to negative and despairing feelings but it also means that human journeys are long and complex. Be patient.

Simple things like not judging, devaluing or stereotyping help a lot. There are good things about being gay. Talk about them. Gays are not always a problem. It can be a gift but, in saying that, we should never underestimate the struggle gay people have.

Every child deserves to be seen as more than a sexual problem. That's why it is important to maintain good, loving, understanding, contact, even when you can't approve or understand everything your child is doing. Be prepared to respect their view even if it differs from yours.

Most of all don't blame yourself, don't blame your child, don't blame God.

Remember This

God won't ask what kind of car you drove,
But He'll ask how many people you drove who didn't have a car.
God won't ask the size of your house,
But He'll ask how many people you welcomed into your home.
God won't ask about the clothes you had in your wardrobe, but
He'll ask how many others you helped to clothe.
God won't ask about your social status;
He will ask how it affected your treatment of others.
God won't ask how many material possessions you had,
But He'll ask if they dictated your life.
God won't ask what your highest salary was,
But He'll ask if you compromised your character to obtain it.
God won't ask how much overtime you worked,
But He'll ask how much your overtime truly benefited your family.
God won't ask how many promotions you received,
But He'll ask how much encouragement you gave to others.
God won't ask what your job title was,
But He'll ask if you performed it to the best of your ability.
God won't ask what you did to help yourself,
But He'll ask what you did to help others.
God won't ask how many friends you had,
But He'll ask how much you were a friend to other people
God won't ask what you did to protect your rights,
But he'll ask what you did to protect the rights of others.
God won't ask in what neighbourhood you lived,
But He'll ask how you treated your neighbours.
God won't ask about the colour of your skin,
But He'll ask about the content of your Character.

Thank God For These Priests

I was delighted to get a lovely letter from a person who had some good things to say about the priesthood. 'I always read your column on Sundays and only for it I wouldn't buy the *Sunday World* at all. Thank you for writing on so many interesting topics.' That's how the letter began and it's always a good start. But the more serious topic surfaced immediately.

'On reading your article on good priests I just had to write to you. I agree there are many good priests out there but we don't hear about their good work. Last year my mother was diagnosed with cancer, her time was short. My dad had died three years previously and the priest in the Parish was very good to us.

'With my mother it was different. Thankfully we could nurse her at home and so the priests began calling when they heard about her illness. There was a parish priest, a young curate and a semi-retired priest in his 80's. Each one came, chatted with my mother, prayed with her and were so good to her throughout her sickness. But it was in her last days that we really felt privileged to experience their kindness.

'The young priest himself was helpful. He called each day during her last week with us; this wasn't because he wasn't busy, as there seemed to be no end to the funerals at that particular time. I was feeling angry with God but he always listened to my anguish and was supportive. He made my mother feel so cherished.

'My mother died on a Sunday night and the young priest called early in the day and again that evening realising my mother's time was short. He said he would be back at midnight. My mother died at 10.30 and he arrived back at 11.15, said prayers with us, had tea and was a great comfort to us. The next morning he was back again and gave us all the support he could.

'As long as I live I will never forget the kindness of these priests at such a sad time in our lives. We don't read about these good men but if they were stepping out of line it would be splashed all over the papers.

'I most certainly don't condone what some priests have done but they are in the minority and people should realise this. Keep up the good work (Grateful Parishioner)'

Who Am I, Lord?

While praying one day a woman asked, 'Who Are You Lord?'

He answered, 'I Am.' 'But who is I Am?' she said

And He replied… 'I Am Love, I Am Peace,

I am Grace, I Am Joy,

I Am The Way, Truth, and The Light…

I Am The Comforter,

I am Strength, I Am Safety,

I am Shelter, I Am Power, I Am The Creator,

I Am The Beginning And The End,

I Am The Most High.'

The girl with tears in her eyes looked

Toward Heaven and said

'Now I understand. But Lord, who am I?'

Then God tenderly wiped the tears

From her eyes and whispered,

'You are Mine'

Nobody Is a Lost Cause in God's Eyes

Has the Catholic Church become a church of convenience? Are its services merely used as a mark of respectability? An excuse for social gatherings with no real meaning and less commitment for our newly rich, 'I'm not very religious, really' clientele? Is it not time to stop the hypocrisy?

These are just some of the questions people inside and outside the Church are asking seriously as the 'New Ireland' boasts about its 'freedom' from the shackles of religious oppression.

People who never appear at Church, critics argue, want to be married with all the trimmings, white dress and all, even though they have been living together for years.

They want their children – when they eventually arrive – baptised, despite the fact that they have no intention of bringing those same children to Mass and couldn't teach them a prayer to save their lives.

They'll want to dress them up for Communion and Confirmation, and then announce that they never go to Church or Communion with the children.

And when the time comes, they'll want a Church funeral with favourite tunes and poetry and speeches from friends.

If a priest doesn't play along with all of this, he's the worst in the world. If he questions Faith, or Practice or Honesty or Commitment, he's a died in the wool conservative who could find himself talked about disparagingly on gossipy phone-ins and condemned high-handedly in columns and letters to the editor, God protect us from all harm.

Frequently, after a wedding or baptism now, the posh will parrot, 'Lovely service, Reverend', a sure give-away. No regular churchgoer would ever say that.

Would it not be more honest to maintain some semblance of integrity and insist on a proper commitment to Church basics before allowing people to 'use' God's house?

Increasingly those who do give their time and energy to church activities feel used by those who come to Church only when it suits them.

A-la-carte Catholics, as they are sometimes called, are much discussed in Church circles these days. And increasingly, those same part-time practitioners are questioning their own 'abuse' of Church services.

One told me recently that their experiences in Germany opened their eyes. There, apparently, you officially declare what your religion is – if any.

The government collects a religion tax from you and sends it on to the church of your choice. The tax pays for your services in the church at a time of need.

They thought it was a good idea because nothing concentrates the modern Irish mind like money. If you pay, you're more likely to pray, they implied.

There's a lot to be said for circling the wagons and, acting with integrity and honesty (those two words again), pruning those half-hearted Christians out of the church. Does scripture not imply as much by saying 'because you are neither hot nor cold, I will vomit you out of my mouth'?

Is that really the way forward?

No way, if you ask me.

I admit it is disheartening when people blatantly 'use' you. They demand baptisms and weddings and blessings on second relationships even though you know they snigger at your life-style.

And, yes, it is depressing when most young people see no point going to Church. The temptation is to come the heavy and clobber them with 'if you don't keep the rules, get out of the club'.

But then humility and good sense take over.

The church is not a club. Never was and never will be.

The Christ I know would never crush the bruised reed. I see it as my duty to help people find Christ, not high-handedly dump them out of the church.

For many, it may well be merely a matter of custom to have special events marked with a religious service. But I also know for certain that

God uses those occasions to get through to even the most cynical of hearts.

The church could stand on its dignity and exclude those it deems unworthy. Many of its members are convinced she should. I don't agree, because Christ came to bring peace to all people of good will and I'm not the judge.

You cannot run the church like a club or a business. Her mission is one of service, not oppression. There must always be an opportunity for God's grace to work. Nobody is a lost cause in God's eyes.

Conversion is always possible. And if they want to involve the church in the significant moments of their lives, for whatever reason, it is not beyond the grace of God to touch their hearts.

In short, I believe in the basic goodness of people, even when they don't believe it themselves.

On Turning 80

Today, Dear Lord, I am 80 and there is so much I haven't done,
I hope, Dear Lord, You will let me live until I'm 81.
But then if I haven't finished all I want to do
Would You let me stay a while until I'm 82.
So many places I want to go, so very much to see,
Do You think You could manage to make it 83?
The world is changing very fast there is much in store,
I'd like it very much to live until I'm 84.
And if by then I'm still alive I'd like to stay 'til 85.
More planes will be up in the air, so I'd really like to stick,
and see what happens to the world when I am 86.
I know, Dear Lord, it's much to ask, and it must be nice in heaven
But I would really like to stay until I'm 87.
I know by then I won't be fast and sometimes will be late,
But it would be so pleasant, to be around at 88.
I will have seen many things and had a wonderful time,
So I'm sure that I'll be willing to leave at 89.....maybe.

Learning From The Handicapped

The lessons we learn from the handicapped are of major importance.

Since Mother Teresa died, Jean Vanier is everyone's idea of what a living saint should be. He has devoted his life to caring for, and learning from, the broken and the handicapped.

Yet when I have spoken to him, he has made me feel uncomfortable. His holiness, his dedication, challenge me to look at the futility of my own life. Mother Teresa had exactly the same effect on me.

Vanier was born in Geneva in 1928. He's the son of a former Governor General of Canada, George Vanier.

His father was Ambassador to France during World War II where Jean Vanier saw inmates arriving from concentration camps who looked like skeletons. That vision marked him for life.

The evil human beings perpetrate on other human beings, led him to study philosophy in an effort to find an answer. Even though he was successful, his life demanded something more.

Vanier was also an officer in the Royal Navy and in the Canadian Navy. So in 1950 he resigned and joined a small community of students, mostly lay, to work with the poor in France. Their aim was to foster prayer and study. At one point in his life he wanted to be a priest but he recognised his particular calling as a layman.

Eventually he bought a small dilapidated house called L'Arche, (which means the Ark - Noah's Ark). There he welcomed two mentally handicapped men to share his home with him. It was the beginning of the hugely successful L'Arche communities.

It is a system which pairs a person who has a disability with a person who hasn't. The aim is to encourage people rejected by society and to give them a place.

Vanier Communities received international attention in the mid 80's when Fr Henri Nouwen, a Catholic priest whose spiritual books have sold millions, settled in a L'Arche community in Canada. Nouwen had been searching for peace all his life without success but it was in

L'Arche that he found his true home.

There are now 104 L'Arche Communities in 30 countries on five continents.

Vanier has the brain of a philosopher but the heart of a saint. He frequently talks about one of the original members of L'Arche who taught him the value of touch:

'He does not understand much, but he does understand whether we touch him with love. Our bodies are called to be instruments of grace. We must learn to touch with tenderness. Touch has been sexualised in our culture, but it is so vitally important to reveal to people their value and give them security.'

Henri Nouwen wrote, 'Handicapped people are not only poor, they also reveal to us our own poverty. They cry in anguish "Do you love me?" and "Why have you forsaken me?" When we are confronted with that cry… we are forced to look at our own terrible loneliness.'

Both men are modern day saints.

Hope

If you can look at the sunset and smile,then you still have hope.

If you can find beauty in the colors of a small flower,
then you still have hope.

If you can find pleasure in the movement of a butterfly,
then you still have hope.

If the smile of a child can still warm your heart,
then you still have hope.

If you can see the good in other people,then you still have hope.

If the rain breaking on a roof top can still lull you to sleep,
then you still have hope.

If the sight of a rainbow still makes you stop and stare in wonder,
then you still have hope.

Ten Commandments to Get You Back to Church

From the several thousand letters a year I receive, it is obvious most of you think the present church structures and strictures are at best irrelevant.

I therefore have sifted out your top ten suggestions about the Church. Ten tips to bring the punters back, as one of you put it.

I. Get Real.

Stop living in the past. Don't tell us how things used to be, with the implication that we should return to the good old days. They weren't that good. This is our new world and we are not going back. We are delighted to be free of those stifling hypocritical times. Brighten up and come and join us in the real world. We are a lot happier here than you are there.

II. Settle on Essentials.

We don't believe in indulgences, out-dated prayers, phoney miracles and those pathetic pilgrimages. They mean nothing to us and they're not important anyway. Older folk love them, that's fair enough. We have a different spiritual side to us. We want a religion that is practical, that allows us to help others and get things done. We pray in times of need and in our way. Help us to do it better. Tell us about a God who cares for us, loves us, encourages us. Sort out what is essential to our Faith. Peripheral devotions and sexual morality are not the only issues that count.

III. Be fair to women.

You are hypocrites when you say you value women. You don't. Women don't have a say, are powerless, cannot be ordained ('Don't even discuss it,' the Pope says), will never be in leadership, and worst of all are patronised with inanities like 'You're the backbone of the Church.'

In fact power is held by ageing, under-active celibates, some of whom are good men, but most of whom are paralysed by fear. Women are not trusted. Not respected. Not encouraged. Women are second-class citizens. Nothing will happen until this changes.

IV. Allow Priests to choose whether they wish to marry or be celibate.
Encourage them to marry if it makes them more happy, more relevant, more natural, more healthy men. Take a look at the candidates joining up these days. They are few in number, many are under-developed, right-wing, tyrants in the making, escapees from the real world, seeking comfort in certainty and power, and too often either are openly or latently gay. You couldn't expect a normal young man in his right senses to waste his life with that lot, especially since he can serve God better as a loving, devoted parent. Get real. Give us normal, healthy human beings as priests.

V. People are more important than institutions.
The church will survive without your back-to-the-wall defences of it. It's not more important than the struggling people who are the Church. Isn't that precisely what was so different with Christ? He put love before law.

If people wish to share the Eucharist, encourage them to do so, even if they are not perfect. Help people to grow through the sacraments rather than using the sacraments as weapons. Stop abusing power by trying to herd people like sheep. Let them choose who they would like to help them through the important journeys of their life – baptism, marriage, death and where to worship. Respect their journey, their intelligence, their goodness.

VI. Encourage Goodness no matter where you find it, especially in those who can't believe.
Help people experiment with worship. Encourage them to go to other faiths and see God and goodness in those congregations. Help people to discover God's goodness within. Highlight their different gifts rather than force everyone to be as brainwashed, and perhaps as brain dead, as we are. Don't expect them to be at your church every week. Their world is bigger than yours and if you are humble enough you might be lucky enough to share the beauty of their new, fresh, wonderful open-mindedness.

VII. Admit you got things wrong.
You're not always right and we know it. Even the Pope attempts to apologise for the brutality and sinfulness of the Church. Why should you feel obliged to defend the indefensible? You don't have all the

answers. You don't even have the questions. We don't expect you to be infallible. We dismiss you as proud little dictators when we see you playing 'god'. We can admire you as a struggling sinner.

Stop covering up the sins of the Church. We know there are good people in leadership in churches. But there are also child abusers, power freaks and sick, sad misfits. It's time to apologise, open up, and pay up. If you want respect you've got to earn it.

VIII. Ask professionals how to make the masses and liturgies more acceptable and less boring.

You are driving us mad and away. You drone on and on about a world we don't know and can't identify with. Sometimes on special occasions we love Mass. It can mean so much to us. But we won't go every Sunday simply to go though a ritual that is obviously meaningless to you, never mind us. Make us feel welcome, happy and loved.

And do we really need to go there every week anyway? Are there not other ways we could pray and find God within ourselves and within our worlds? Spare us the long-winded sermons and horrible singing of platitudinous hymns?

IX. Tell us about the God of the second chance.

When our marriages and commitments are successful they're marvellous. But they don't always work out. Usually it's nobody's fault. And if we get a chance of real love the second time around, we know it's from God because God is love. So why do you insist on punishing us by making us feel like lepers in Church? We feel safe with God but not with you in your Church. Think about that.

We know and accept that abortion is wrong, but make some effort to understand the struggles of people who see it differently, and the sheer hell some pregnant women go though.

Help us raise our children with dignity rather than condemn us because we don't plan our families in precisely the way you want us to. Get out of our beds and realise that how we share our love is our own business.

X. Give up power.

Do you have to spend so much time controlling Catholic schools? Do you have to spend so much energy controlling boards of management? Do you have to insist on dictating to us about how we should marry, live, pray?

Why should you tell us how much we should pay when we don't have any say in how it's spent? Could we not be free to choose our parish and to have a say in how it's run? Why are you so afraid of us? In 10 years many of you will be dead and we'll have to run the parishes anyway. Train us now and the Faith may live. Treat us with disdain and the harsh judgement will be on you. In a few short years we should be able to choose our priests and bishops, as the people did for centuries before control freaks got their way. Share power. A power that's rightfully ours anyway.

Life is too short and Faith too important for us to spend our lives fighting. Together we have something precious and your fear is killing the Spirit because you won't change and come to live in our real world. But it's never too late to start.

Still More Hope

If you meet new people with a trace of excitement and optimism,
then you still have hope.
If you give people the benefit of a doubt,
then you still have hope.
If you offer your hand in friendship to others that
have touched your life, then you still have hope.
If receiving an unexpected card or letter still brings a
pleasant surprise, then you still have hope.
If the suffering of others still fills you with pain and frustration,
then you still have hope.
If you refuse to let a friendship die, or accept that it
must end, then you still have hope.
If you look forward to a time or place of quiet and
reflection, then you still have hope.

Only The Laity Can Save The Church

Here I am going on again about the deeply ingrained evil of clericalism destroying the credibility of our beautiful church. It is a kind of clericalism which is not confined to the Catholic church but is more evident there.

Because of it, one essential point has been missed and no amount of rearranging the deck chairs will camouflage it.

The point is this: The church will be saved by its laity or it will not be saved at all. Clerics need to be redeemed by the very laity whose talents we have trifled with for centuries. A dedicated, committed lay people are the only hope the church has. It is the laity who will determine if we clerics are serious in our efforts to accept responsibility for the sex abuse scandals.

The most hopeful sign in the present day church is that many lay people are still willing to throw us a life-line if we are humble enough to grasp it.

In return the laity will demand a share in decision making within the church which is their right by baptism.

After centuries of the laity being accountable to the clergy, true balance will be restored when catholics demand greater accountability from their leaders.

In America in particular the voice of the Catholic laity has come to the fore. Reform must begin with the way leaders in parishes and in the dioceses are chosen. Until this is changed all other attempts at reform will remain toothless.

Genuine leadership can never be imposed. It's earned. Leaders, whether of the parish or of the diocese, will be chosen through prayerful and thoughtful consensus within the community.

Careerism, a real scandal in the Church today, has to be uprooted. Pastoral competence should be the main criterion.

The final point is this. The church was never meant to be, and cannot be, two peoples - the clergy and the laity. We are one people of God.

It is a contradiction in terms to have a church where there is a privileged class. As the Vatican Council put it: 'There is one call to holiness that applies to all the baptised. There is one ministry to the world that all share.'

How to Make a Child into a Delinquent

1. Begin at infancy to give the child everything he wants.
2. When he picks up bad language, laugh at him.
3. Never give him any spiritual training. Wait until he is eighteen, then let him 'decide for himself'.
4. Avoid the use of the word 'wrong'. It may develop a guilt complex.
5. Pick up everything he leaves lying around – books, shoes, clothes etc.
6. Let him read any printed matter he can get his hands on.
7. Quarrel frequently in the presence of your children. In this way they will not be too shocked when the home is broken up later.
8. Give a child all the spending money he wants. Why should he have things as tough as you had them?
9. Satisfy his every craving for food, drink and comfort. Denial may lead to harmful frustration.
10. Take his part against neighbours, teachers and policemen.
11. When he gets into real trouble, apologise for yourself by saying, 'I could never do anything with him.'
12. Prepare yourself for a life of grief.

Anon.

The Church We Have, The Church We Need

I met a friend from my past recently. He's a happily married man with two grown children. He's been successful in his profession and will retire shortly.

He and his wife have plans to work voluntarily for their community and to live a simple, comfortable, relaxed life.

They are both spiritual people who have adjusted to change well. They are obviously happy, fulfilled and at peace.

My friend was once a priest like myself, only he was much better than me. He retired from active ministry and married the woman he loved. It was a difficult decision for both of them – and for their families too. Looking at them now, it was truly a holy, inspired choice on their life's journey.

Had my friend stayed he would have been a good priest too, but his life would have been very different. For a start, there would not have been any possibility of retirement.

He would be working not less than 12 hectic hours a day, seven days a week and be on call 24/7. He would typically live on his own, cater for himself and be in charge of a parish with multiple churches and schools. He would have given the best years of his life to the priesthood in the certainty that in middle and old age, another crop of capable curates would do the donkey work for him.

Now he would find himself doing the donkey work with not a curate in sight. He would be a good, dedicated priest, but tired, overworked and, if he thinks at all, frustrated. In other words, he would be part of the priesthood in crisis.

He would not be the happy, mature, emotionally healthy man he now is, thanks to his own openness and his wife's wisdom and love.

Many of his classmates tell him what it's like to be a priest today.

Looking around, a normal priest is aware that a large proportion of his parish doesn't attend church regularly. They come for baptisms, weddings and funerals. They don't need the church at other times. He knows he's irrelevant to their lives – most of the time anyway. They haven't lost faith in God – they have just given up on the church as they experience it.

The young see him as a relic from the past. They have no sense of what all this religion thing means. It's not that they are switched off by the church, it's more that they were never switched on. So much for Catholic schools with their so-called Catholic ethos.

He knows that married couples make up their own minds about sexual morality. They plan their families themselves as effectively as they can and he knows they are right, but dare not say so.

It's the 'sin' no one mentions; an unnecessary battle that couldn't be won. There'll be no dialogue, no discussion, just silence. It's a good example of common sense from the people and communal denial by the church. From the Church's position, a most unhealthy state of affairs.

Most sensible priests still try to involve every section of the community, but recognise that women are more disillusioned than priests are.

Women's ordination cannot even be discussed – proof that there is no sustainable argument against it – and anyway it's taken for granted that women have no rights, but if they ask celibate men nicely, they may be given some 'privileges.' Actually all lay people tell me they have similar experiences.

When he speaks with other priests, he finds two distinct trends. One group, usually the very old and the few young, see no problem. Their way of coping is to deny the problem exists. He understands the old men because they'll hang on for a few years and die peacefully. Who could argue with that?

The young baffle him because he can't understand why they became priests in today's climate and how they came out of training with such blinkered, intransigent views.

Even in his day he was taught that faith is not a static condition but a way of being on pilgrimage. Ideals have to be proclaimed, but nobody lives them fully on this earth. It's common sense and good pastoral care.

He knows there won't be a dramatic surge of vocations. He willingly spends days at conferences discussing the latest in-word 'clustering.' He'll cut back on Masses, stand in for a neighbouring priest who gets sick and help out with penitential services which he knows are of little use. When he allows himself to think at all, he knows the game's up. And if he had the courage, he would tell his clustering meeting what he really feels:

- It's not the number of Masses that counts. It's the quality of them.
- Our preaching is out of date. Our experiences don't match our congregation's. We live in two different worlds. A good man expounding irrelevant spirituality. Good people dying in a spiritual famine.
- There should be general absolution of sins on special occasions. There is no need to stick with a formula which was once helpful, but is no longer meaningful. Churches are full of repentant people if only we were brave enough to reach out to them in a compassionate way. There is no limit to God's compassion. With God there is no such thing as compassion fatigue.
- Priests don't have to be single and celibate. If some want it that way let them choose it. But don't confine the gift of priesthood to males with imposed vows of celibacy.
- Allow priests to marry and also ordain men who are married.
- Every living parish/community has many good, qualified and willing married men and women who would give a definite number of years to presiding at Eucharist and to serving their community as priests. In the early church, leaders were always chosen from within, not imposed from without. Use the gifts God is giving us.
- If we believe the Mass is central, then the canon law which determines who can be ordained a priest should be changed. Where canon law is an obstacle to the Gospel message, choose the Gospel and change the law.
- Make a stand against the imposition of 'safe' bishops from Rome. Fight against those who undo the reforms of the Second Vatican Council which was the work of the Spirit. Those who oppose it are following a bad spirit.
- Don't make a virtue of passivity. It is not 'loyal' to suppress or ignore real problems. It is the unforgivable sin.
- Listen to the people. Give them real power. Trust them with money. Trust their commitment. They have a right and duty to talk about what disturbs them.

The Vatican Council said so over 40 years ago. 'By reason of the knowledge, competence or pre-eminence which they have, the laity are empowered – indeed sometimes obliged – to manifest their opinion on those things which pertain to the good of the Church' *(Lumen Gentium).*

- Invite all those who left the priesthood to marry, back to active ministry. Thousands would willingly come back, enriching the priesthood and entire church with new gifts and experiences.
- Welcome women to genuine leadership roles. Allow them to preach the Word at Mass. They are forbidden to do so now. Even women who train seminarians to preach are themselves prevented from giving an actual homily. How stupid is that?
- Get real and find new ways to get bums back on church seats. It can be done. Good preachers and lively liturgies still enthral, inspire and attract.
- Scrap the seniority rule in most dioceses, whereby a man, if he lives long enough, will be imposed on a parish, no matter how unstable or unsuitable he is. It's institutionalism gone mad.
- Learn a new sexual morality from married people. At present, no matter what we say, we really do believe sex is bad. Look at the damage we've done to ourselves and others living out that falsehood. Sex is good and a gift from God.
- Let the laity have a say in who they want as their priest/leader and let both priests and laity appoint their Bishop.

These are just some of the unmentionables we should be discussing. Honest conversation and discussion can only bring good. There are still good people out there who want a church they can own and be proud of. Some of us narrow-minded, frightened, jaded clerics are strangling the Spirit and killing the Church. A vociferous and powerful right wing laity is no asset either.

I don't expect you to agree with all of what I've said. But I've got so much encouragement from most laity and so much grief from some clerics recently that I've been thinking, praying, reflecting and pondering the future.

I don't mean to hurt anyone, but I make no apology for the challenge offered.

Things You Can Learn from a Dog

- Allow the experience of fresh air and the wind in your face to be pure ecstasy.
- When loved ones come home, always run to greet them.
- When it's in your best interest, practice obedience.
- Let others know when they've invaded your territory.
- Take naps and stretch before rising.
- Run, romp and play daily.
- Eat with gusto and enthusiasm.
- Be loyal.
- Never pretend to be something you're not.
- If what you want lies buried, dig until you find it.
- When someone is having a bad day, be silent, sit close by and nuzzle them gently.
- Thrive on attention and let people touch you.
- Avoid biting when a simple growl will do.
- On hot days, drink lots of water and lie under a shady tree.
- When you're happy, dance around and wag your entire body.
- No matter how often you're scolded, don't buy into the guilt thing and pout… run right back and make friends.
- Bond with your pack.
- Delight in the simple joy of a long walk.

Learning to Accept Who You Are

To realise you're gay can be a traumatising moment even in today's enlightened Ireland.

It is a shock and often a relief for the person themselves. For families it can be the most trying experience they'll face. Here, in his own words, is one man's journey to acceptance.

'I've read your column through the years and perceived it as a compassionate and non-judgemental avenue for all sorts of people to share their experiences, good, bad and indifferent, with the wider public.

'Perhaps it could help other people in my predicament – let them know that they are not alone.

'Maybe in some small way it will soften people's attitudes and hopefully it will exorcise some of my own inner demons.'

That is how the writer, who obviously wishes to remain anonymous, began his letter. Stay with his story to the end.

'What really pisses me off,' he continued, 'is when people equate sexuality with choice, and the natural corollary, blame.

'Choice! I chose to give up everything I know and love, everything I feel a part of – my family, my friends, those who think they know me, my home, my background and my memories. And for what?

'To stand alone against hostility and uncertainty and be labelled as queer, a faggot, a puff, by those of you with preconceived bigoted stereotypes of what a gay person is.

'I chose to leave the most wonderful girl I or anybody else could ever hope to meet, radiant in personality as well as simple beauty, the person I grew through adolescence with, grew to love and who became my best friend.

'And why? Because every day I was becoming more aware that I could never make her ultimately happy, happiness I knew she deserved.

'In reality, I could never offer her an honest explanation as to why what looked so right to everyone else, and should have been to me, was in fact being daily eroded by a conscious awakening that I was different.

'I chose to live a life embroiled in secrecy, shut out my closest friends and family from the hardest thing I would ever have to deal with, and face it alone to arrive at a situation which I would initially deny, then subsequently fight and eventually grudgingly accept.

'I chose not to let my family hear me cry myself to sleep, or to explain when I erupted in sudden bursts of anger directed at those closest to me.

'Damn them! Why couldn't they see the inner turmoil that was shredding my soul? Unfortunately for those of you with easily acquired opinions I, and others like me, did not choose this shit – that I as an individual am different in a 'normal' society.

'It is easier for you to label someone without looking behind the defining tag you've just given them.

'You see choice doesn't really play a part in the equation. The element of choice has been removed as an option because, as a 23-year-old male, I know I wouldn't be happy in a 'normal' relationship.

'No. I didn't choose this but it is a constituent element of my being, one which is difficult, if not sometimes impossible to accept.

'Why? Because I considered myself to be a good kid, the one who routinely served mass, felt a sense of compassion towards those less well off. I did well at school because I wanted to make my parents proud and one day be able to give them the things that they sacrificed so their children could see a better life than what they had known.

'I prayed regularly because deep down I knew there was a Divine Authority, this higher power that would see me okay.

'I suppose a child's naïve belief that if you were good, good things would befall you.

'How could it be then that I was gay? After all this is grossly wrong and an affront to the dignity of our Catholic teaching.

'But on the other hand, God made us all and He loves us all.

'Rationalising this didn't and still doesn't add up. If God made us all, why did He make some of us different and if He loves us all why would He let some of us face into this abyss of pain and uncertainty alone.

'Neither was it something that I learned. Coming from a West of Ireland rural upbringing, I had plenty of female interest from adolescence, through college and still have. I was generally considered as 'one of the lads'.

'I still pray but now I pray for different things. I pray that I myself may have the ability to accept the things I cannot change and be at ease with who I am.

'I've been lucky enough to meet a truly good person; gentle, kind and caring.

'He has restored my faith in many things. I hope that the attitudes imprinted on my own heart and mind by my upbringing, and the societal attitudes that I've been exposed to, will not stunt my own ability to love and maintain this relationship.

'I pray that no young person should have to face into this struggle alone.

'Try talking to somebody. Anybody. A counsellor, maybe even a friend you think will understand.

'Only recently I had the courage to tell someone very close to me.

'Sharing this was an over powering relief and brought us so much closer.

'She told me she could now finally look into my eyes and see me. She could understand things that in the past didn't make sense.

'Like, why on nights out I might steal away into the background of whatever jovial gathering I was in and stand alone in some dismal corner where the dazzling lights couldn't cast their happy glow over me.

'I pray that young people will be more aware. Understand the pain a simple remark may cause. Never under or overestimate your friends, and be sensitive to who they might be.

'I pray that parents will know and understand their children as they succumb to the hostility of adolescence and growing up.

'Mothers and fathers: equip yourselves with the knowledge of who your son or daughter is.

'As for my own family, I pray I will one day have the strength and courage to tell them and they will accept and love me.

'I hope I will remain part of their lives, able to share with them in the future, things that I couldn't in the past.

'God grant us all the ability to accept the things we cannot change.'

‘I’m Grateful for Cancer’

How can you help when somebody is told they have cancer? That was the question I posed in my newspaper column. I made some suggestions and asked for help.

Charles Murray is in a good position to help. He has lived in London all his life. A few years ago his wife died suddenly as a result of a clot. The shock and stress had a significant effect on Charles and his three children.

A few months later he himself was rushed to hospital with a clot in his leg. This time, thankfully, the doctors were able to save him. But that was not all.

‘Two months after that I underwent several medical tests including a biopsy and was diagnosed with Hodgkin’s Lymphoma. Leaving the hospital I was in a state of shock. My three children were married and I was coming home to an empty house. Looking back, informing my family was not easy,’ Charles writes. ‘There were many tears and I still felt guilty because they were trying to come to terms with the loss of their mother only 8 months earlier. I felt I was placing a heavy burden on them with my illness.

‘I found the delay from being diagnosed to receiving treatment difficult to accept. I was only being selfish for I was not the only one waiting for treatment. The treatment started in June. It consisted of four hours chemotherapy every two weeks. My hair began to part company with me and in no time I was looking like Kojak – completely bald. The treatment lasted for nine months.

‘When I was diagnosed, and after telling my family, I spoke to my parish priest. He put my name on the sick list in the weekly Newsletter and it remained there for the full nine months of treatment… I now realise the power of prayer. I was not alone but had the parish, my family, friends in England and friends in Ireland to support me. And there were prayers too from the nuns of the Poor Clare Order at the local convent…’

The outcome was that Charles was given the all-clear. But apart from the necessity of prayers, he had some other helpful remarks about his illness.

'Looking back I found that some people could be very hurtful, with remarks about my weight loss. At the same time the hospital provided me with a special wig to keep my head warm and - sadly – some people thought this very funny. It was difficult to turn the other cheek.

'Now I'm putting on weight again and had my first haircut a few weeks ago. These same people never say how well I'm looking. My advice to people diagnosed with cancer is to tell everyone they meet, and ask them to pray for you. Don't isolate yourself.'

Charles makes a number of points very well. It does help to have people praying for you. But it also helps if we could be a little more sensitive. Laughing at wigs when people need them, or making fun of weight loss, is not very helpful. There is always a bright side though and Charles finishes by saying, 'Having being diagnosed with cancer has opened up a new chapter in my life for which I am very grateful.'

Grateful for cancer? Now there's something special!

Cancer Sufferers: A Few More Words on How to Help Them

What is the best way to react when someone you know has cancer? What can you say? What can you do? If I knew the answer I wouldn't make as many mistakes as I do. I often write down a list of 'dos' and 'don'ts' for myself and I'll share some with you.

Many people still hear the diagnosis of cancer as a death sentence.

Sometimes we can't cope with such stark reminders of our own mortality. And because we haven't come to terms with the possibility of death we think the person suffering hasn't either. So we pretend that everything is as it was. That's not helpful.

Let's be positive. One out of two cancer patients will be alive, disease free, five or more years from this day. For some forms of cancer the cure rate is as high as nine out of ten.

There are many special factors which play a definitive role in survival – where the diseased cells are, the stage at which the cancer is discovered and the ability of the patient to respond to new therapies.

Emotional attitudes have a powerful influence on the body's immune and restorative powers. Positive thinking won't cure cancer, but it sure does help.

Good positive emotions like hope, faith, love, laughter and a will to live, do have a curative effect on the body. And that's where friends come in.

When someone you love has cancer there are ways you can help, just as there are attitudes you should avoid.

Don't think of the patient as the cancer victim. Patients are always surviving cancer, recovering from it and trying their best to make every day as life-filled as possible. They are not victims, they are survivors.

They want us to be understanding, to listen, encourage and allow the sick person to be in charge. They may not want to go partying every night, but they are part of a living world.

Don't blame them for getting cancer. 'When I think of all those years you smoked' or, 'Didn't you examine your breasts regularly,' are not the kind of remarks to make. The patient has wrestled with those questions a million times.

Equally bad are the suggestions of cures and, worse still, overburdening people with relics. So many patients exhaust themselves with novenas. Try to convince them to say a few short prayers. That's enough. Isn't their suffering the best possible prayer?

Don't ask, 'Are you in remission?' It's amazing how often that question pops into your mind. Bite your tongue and don't say it. It implies they have only a brief time to live.

Those who work constantly with cancer patients recognise typically unhelpful types:

- First there's the cheer leader: 'We can lick this thing, you'll be right as rain in no time.'
- There's overprotection: 'Whatever you do, you're not to lift that vacuum cleaner. Just lie down and rest.'
- Equally disconcerting is the opposite which ignores the sickness. 'Shall we plan a mountain-climbing holiday just after Christmas?'
- Then there's the temptation to chat incessantly. The patient might want nothing more than someone to sit with. Let the patient control your help.

Even the most highly trained make mistakes. I know I have been trying to learn the art of journeying with the sick for more than 30 years now. I still feel utterly inadequate.

The person who has cancer feels isolated and, incredible as it seems, there are still people who behave as if cancer is contagious. So it's important to visit, to sit close, to touch, to hug to be comforting and reassuring.

Be sensitive to how the patient is at this particular time of this particular day. A patient may be bright and chatty in the morning and be dead beat at lunch time.

Because patients become actors they often behave in the way they think you want them to behave. You need to give them permission to be themselves.

Be careful too about the ordinary things. Make sure the glass of water is within reach. Ask them how their pillows are. Make them comfortable.

If the patient really trusts you, they'll talk about their fears. That may set all sorts of emotions going on within you. However, if they want to talk about death, let them. If they want to talk about pain, talk about it. If they have doubts, especially religious doubts, allow them to have them. Accept them as they are.

Quite frequently I find that a patient's biggest fear isn't the fear of death. Often it's the fear of being alone. A little reassurance on that point can be the most comforting words a patient will ever hear.

There is good news on the medical front too. Breast cancer is the most common cancer among women, according to the World Health Organisation. Most women, when diagnosed early, recover from it. Death rates have fallen by 20 per cent in the last ten years alone.

I realise I've only scratched the surface. But it's a start.

SOME WISDOM FROM GRANDAD

- Whether a man winds up with a nest egg, or a goose egg, depends a lot on the kind of chick he marries.
- Trouble in marriage often starts when a man gets so busy earning his salt, that he forgets his sugar.
- Too many couples marry for better or worse, but not for good.
- When a man marries a woman, they become one. The trouble starts when they try to decide which one.
- If a man has enough horse sense to treat his wife like a thoroughbred, she will never turn into an old nag.
- On anniversaries, the wise husband always forgets the past – but never the present.
- Many girls like to marry a military man – he can cook, sew, make beds, is in good health, and he's already used to taking orders.
- Eventually you will reach a point when you stop lying about your age, and start bragging about it.

Two Voices: Abuser and Abused

The Abuser

'I'm out of practice at writing so please excuse this letter. I feel that I need to reply to your article of a few months ago. Like 'Michael' in one of the letters I too was a child abuser. I abused up to eight children who were all young girls around seven to eight-years-old. I simply cannot explain the remorse I am experiencing. For some time at the beginning, I didn't realise that what I was doing was wrong. And needless to say I didn't fully comprehend the damage I was doing to the people I abused.

'I didn't choose to be a child abuser. I now believe it's in my genes. Thank God I managed to control it. How I don't know. I know prayer helped.

'When I was a child I watched my sister being abused. This must have had a huge effect on me. Both of us seem to be really messed up ever since. As far as I know, most of my victims have put it behind them and have become beautiful young women, God bless them. I prayed for them and continue to do so. Unlike Michael I was never convicted. Sometimes I wish I was.'

So far the letter is reasonable enough. But at this point the letter writer, unwittingly perhaps, shows he is not living in the real world. He needs to receive proper counselling. It's obvious that his sexuality is suppressed rather than dealt with healthily.

He continues: 'The reason mature men abuse children, I believe, is that their sexual needs are not being looked after. I'm not making excuses for them but I'm sure you have noticed the immodest dress of many young girls at the present time. It seems to be accepted for girls to go out in public almost naked. It's like a competition to see who can get away with wearing the least.

'My own sexual history is appalling. My needs have been neglected for years.

'Your writer, Michael, is right when he says that the media loves to use this material. Yet look at the amount of porn adverts in the papers. On one page they write about a perv who does something and the next it's full of almost nude pictures.

'This is a time for cleansing. It's a time to expose the filth and rid ourselves of it. If you are a man and you are experiencing sexual problems, what do you do? They say there is help, but is it the right kind of help? Sometimes help can be very hard to find and when one does find it, it may be useless. There are all kind of adverts for health problems and helplines for everything except our problem.

'Is there a helpline for child abusers? I don't think so. It's a very serious problem and yet there is no helpline. You know it takes a lot of courage to own up to something like this. I am appealing to men with sexual difficulties, first of all to accept it and then seek help.'

I understand the writer's frustration, but he should take his own advice and get help for something that is obviously troubling him. I see dangerous signs in his thought patterns.

He concludes by saying quite rightly that victims of sexual abuse should not blame themselves. 'The blame or fault lies entirely with the person who abused you. Try not to be victims all your life, try to put it behind you.'

I use letters like this one from Sean to show that we need to understand the mind of the abuser. I know victims who read this will find it upsetting. But we have to try to work together to overcome the awful evil of abuse of children.

The Abused

'The letter you had in your column from Katie, who was abused, could have been written by myself,' she begins. 'I was abused years ago by my brother. I kept it a secret for 32 years. I could never tell my parents because I loved them so much and it would hurt them. My brother was older than me and was always put on a pedestal but I hated him all my life. I always felt dirty and I had a lot of sickness, including a brain tumour 20 years ago.

'As a result I spent a lot of time in hospital and never went with boys. My mother and father died a few years ago and after my father died I had another brain tumour. After the operation when I came home, I felt very lonely because for the first time in my life I realised I had nobody in this world.

'I simply couldn't cope because I had this tumour to live with on top of the dirty secret. I could not accept that all this could happen to me so one night I got into my car and drove to the river. I locked the car. Before I left I phoned my brother's house and left a message for him.

'I fell asleep in the car and the next thing I knew the gardai were knocking on my window. I had every intention of committing suicide but the gardai took me out of the car. My brother and his wife arrived with the gardai and I was brought back home. My brother kept saying to me that I should go to a mental institution. He said that if I didn't sign the form he would.

'I was going to tell the gardai why I was committing suicide, in front of my brother, but when I looked at his wife I couldn't hurt her. In the end I signed the form and went into the mental hospital.

'I was in the hospital one week and the doctor said I should not be there. I didn't tell him about the abuse. But then I took an overdose of tablets and finished up in the hospital. I had to go for counselling.

'I was getting nowhere and I still had not told about the abuse. I then took another overdose, finished up in hospital and got out again, but went for counselling. One day I was feeling very low when I was with my counsellor and I told everything about the abuse.

'I had to go to my doctor straight away and I told my doctor and he arranged for me to see a counsellor at the Rape Crisis Centre. Later I told my sisters about the abuse but they wouldn't listen to me and they turned their backs on me. Their doors were shut in my face. I was shunned by the whole family and by their children.

'I went to a priest I thought that I could talk to. He gave me a number for the Samaritans. Altogether I took six overdoses and I wrote to my brother asking him to say sorry. I told him I forgave him but he never answered my letters.

'I decided to press charges. I made a statement to the gardai. The relief I got when I did that was unbelievable. The dirty secret was out of my head and I even felt my tumour was gone once one I told it.

'Like Katie, I didn't want to hurt my family or see anyone in jail. No matter how deeply I am hurt, I love my family, but at this stage I wouldn't want them back in my life.

'I lost my dignity, my childhood, my family and I would not wish that on anybody. All I can say now is that, thanks to my counsellor, my doctors, the gardai and some good friends, I am surviving.'

,

What Senior Citizens Are Worth

Did you know that we old folks are worth a fortune? We have silver in our hair, gold in our teeth, stones in our kidneys, lead in our feet and gas in our stomachs! I have become older since I saw you last and a few changes have come into my life. Frankly, I have become a frivolous old woman!! I am seeing six gentlemen every day! As soon as I wake up Will Power helps me out of bed, then I go to see Jimmy Riddle and then it's time for breakfast with Mr. Kellogg followed closely by the refreshing company of Mr Tetley or my other friend whom I only know by his initials, P.G.! Then comes someone I don't like at all – Arthur It is – he knows he is not welcome, but he insists on being here and what is more, he stays for the rest of the day. Even then he does not like to stay in one place, so he takes me from joint to joint. After such a hectic day I am glad to get to bed and with Johnny Walker too!!

What a hectic life! Oh yes, I am now flirting with Al Zheimer! The priest called the other day and said that at my age I should be thinking of the hereafter. So I told him I did that all the time. For no matter where I am, the bedroom, the kitchen, the sitting-room or the garden, I ask myself, 'Now what am I here after?' Well, I'll close now and I hope that Will Power is your constant companion too, but do make sure that his friend Emma Royd doesn't creep up on you from behind!! And watching out for the crafty one – Gerry Atric!!!.

Submitted by a senior lady!

Did you Hear the One About the Two Nuns?

Every now and again we need to stretch our minds a little. A mate sent me this and if I'm honest I have to admit I had to say three Hail Marys at the end of it. See if you can do better than I did:-

THERE WERE TWO NUNS….

One of them was know as Sister Mathematical (SM) and the other one was known as Sister Logical (SL). It was getting dark and they were still far away from the convent.

SM: Have you noticed that a man has been following us for the past thirty-eight and a half minutes? I wonder what he wants.

SL: It's logical. He wants to rape us.

SM: Oh no! At this rate he will reach us in fifteen minutes at the most! What can we do?

SL: The only logical thing to do is to walk faster.

SM: It's not working.

SL: Of course it's not working. The man did the only logical thing. He started to walk faster, too.

SM: So, what shall we do? At this rate he will reach us in one minute.

SL: The only logical thing to do is split. You go that way. He cannot follow us both.

So the man decided to follow Sister Logical. Sister Mathematical arrives at the convent and is worried about what has happened to Sister Logical.

Then Sister Logical arrives.

SM: Sister Logical! Thank God you are here! Tell me what happened!

SL: The only logical thing happened. The man couldn't follow us both, so he followed me.

SM: Yes, yes! But what happened then?

SL: The only logical thing happened. I started to run as fast as I could and he started to run as fast as he could.

SM: And?

SL: The only logical thing happened. He reached me.
SM: Oh, dear! What did you do?
SL: The only logical thing to do. I lifted my habit up.
SM: Oh, Sister! What did the man do?
SL: The only logical thing to do. He dropped his pants.
SM: Oh, no! What happened then?
SL: Isn't it logical, Sister? A nun with her dress up can run faster than a man with his pants down.

And for those of you who thought it would be dirty, say three Hail Marys!

People In Your Life

People come into your life for a reason, a season, or a lifetime. When you figure out which one it is, you will know what to do for each person.
When someone is in your life for a *reason*, it is usually to meet a need you have expressed. They have come to assist you through a difficulty, to provide you with guidance and support, to aid you physically, emotionally or spiritually.
They may seem like a Godsend, and they are!
They are there for a reason you need them to bc.
Sometimes they die, sometimes they walk away. So what we must realise is that our need has been met, our desire fulfilled, their work is done. The prayers you sent up have been answered.
When people come into your life for a *season*... it is because your turn has come to share, grow or learn. They bring you an experience of peace, or make you laugh. They may teach you something you have never done. They usually give you an unbelievable amount of joy. Believe it! It is real! But only for a season.

Lifetime friendships teach you *lifetime* lessons; things you must build upon in order to have solid emotional foundations...
Your job is to accept the lesson, love the person, and put what you have learnt to use in all other relationships and areas of your life.

Face to Face With AIDS

A few years ago Aids was supposed to be a disease of the 80s, defeated by medical science. It's no such thing. Sadly Aids is as destructive as ever and could yet destroy the continent of Africa.

So if you know someone with Aids, here are a few tips, from those involved in the ministry, on how best to help.

We don't know everything about Aids, but we do know you have nothing to fear by being physically close to a person with Aids. The virus is not airborne. It's transmitted by direct contact with bodily fluids.

Most of us, despite our best efforts, carry fears and prejudices. But don't carry them into the room with you.

If the person with Aids is a homosexual or if they have contracted it through IV drug abuse, then you'll have feelings about homosexuality and drug abuse which you need to deal with.

But remember that Aids is a disease, not a moral issue. It is an indiscriminate disease. It can and does strike people without regard to age, background, lifestyle or vocation. I've been in a room with people dying from an Aids related illness, one of whom was a priest and the other a joyrider and both of them died beautiful deaths.

If you're particularly close to the person dying, you go through many of the same emotions the dying person goes through. You try to deny it. You bargain with God. You go through the many stages of grief. So you need to pay attention to your own feelings.

To be good for the person with Aids you need to find strength from some other person or group. Nobody walks through the stages of grief in easy and tidy steps. Grieving is a messy business. If you allow yourself to experience your feelings fully, however uncomfortable that may be at the time, you will allow healing into your life.

The best way to help somebody with Aids is to be with them. People with Aids often experience isolation. There is still a stigma about it. They are often shunned by their loved ones too.

You don't need to fuss over them like a mother hen. It's better to allow a person to live the time they have to the fullest and in the way they enjoy best.

If particularly close to the person, the hardest thing you'll have to do is to let go. That doesn't mean abandoning them. It means that their life is not yours to control.

I remember a young man with Aids telling me that, because his mother wanted him to be well, he was forced to hide his illness from her. He tried to hide what was happening to him so that those closest to him wouldn't feel the pain.

Ultimately 'letting go' means that the one you love belongs to a Higher Power. Turn the person over to the care of that Higher Power through prayer and you'll be one step nearer peace.

You need to be grateful. I don't mean that you should be grateful for Aids.

Aids is a devastating disease that we must fight with all the resources we can. But in almost every curse there's a blessing. People with Aids, like any person near to death, can teach us a lot about living. They can tell us about the value of daily living.

Often people with Aids tell me that it has been a blessing to them too. They can look at life differently. They are able to forgive. They can mend fences. They learn about themselves.

And most of them know that when death comes it will bring the ultimate healing.

So be aware of what the person with Aids is telling you. About death. About life. About companionship and compassion. About faith and hope.

Hope that no life is wasted. And that if we live our life on this earth to the full, there is a better life awaiting us.

In the last analysis, it's love, not Aids, which conquers all.

The Simpsons: The only Normal Family on TV?

I can't believe they thought about getting rid of Bart, Homer, Marge, Maggie and Lisa!

What would the world come to? They are the only friends I have left. And despite the fact that they are more popular than ever, some senseless man wanted The Simpsons snuffed out.

Homer and the clan are about the only normal family left on television. Life wouldn't be the same without them.

You may dismiss them as a mere cartoon, but the Windsors, the Bush family, the Kennedys and even the Waltons don't come close to The Simpsons in either popularity or influence.

I don't know of any family with as many dysfunctions who not only make us laugh at ourselves, but pepper every episode with brilliant soundbites of philosophy.

I am a late convert to The Simpsons. But now I drop in on my favourite family at every possible opportunity. You never know what you are going to get. There's slapstick humour, Bart's plain bad manners, Homer's brain-dead stupidity and in the middle of it all some of the best satire on television. Which has prompted American universities to run courses on their wisdom.

Way back in the early 90s they were condemned by George Bush Snr. That really made me look at them. If George Bush thought they were dangerous, then they must have something to offer the real world.

The older Bush wanted to make American families more like the Waltons than The Simpsons. Which just goes to show how utterly sad he was.

Why would anyone want to drop them when they are equally popular on both sides of the Atlantic and can attract world-wide viewing figures of 60 million a week?

They were created in 1987 when the producers of the Tracey Ullman Show commissioned Matt Groening to give them a 30 second filler.

He sketched the cartoon in a matter of minutes and named Marge and

Homer after his own parents. Maggie and Lisa are actually his sisters' names and Bart, as you might expect, is brat jumbled up.

Your favourite Simpson can say a lot about you too. In America Bart is the favourite while old brain-dead Homer is the number one on this side of the Atlantic. That figures. The Americans like the young noisy rebel while we prefer somebody to be fat, drunk, stupid and lovable.

Perhaps what makes the Simpsons really popular is that they are not perfect. Like the rest of us they muddle through somehow.

Without getting too preachy about it, after watching The Simpsons you feel, that for all their faults, they at least care about one another. And there aren't many TV families about which that can be said.

So thank God they're keeping The Simpsons. Without them who would we laugh at if they didn't help us to laugh at ourselves?

Mother Teresa
Live the Life

Life is an opportunity, try to take it.
Life is beauty, admire it.
Life is bliss, savour it.
Life is a dream, make it real.
Life is a challenge, try to confront it.
Life is a duty, complete it.
Life is a game, play it.
Life is precious, protect it.
Life is richness, make a treasure of it.
Life is love, enjoy it.
Life is a mystery, try to reveal it.
Life is a promise, carry it out.
Life is sadness, try to get over it.
Life is a hymn, sing it.
Life is a fight, accept it.
Life is an adventure, run the risk.
Life is felicity, try to deserve it.
Life is life, defend it.

Lusting After New Sins

According to the BBC the seven deadly sins are out of date.

To prove it is true here is a wee test for you. If I were offering you a good meal (so that you could commit at least two deadly sins on the one night) I doubt if you could name all seven for me.

To save your embarrassment the seven deadly sins as of old were these. Anger, pride, envy, gluttony, lust, sloth and greed.

According to the BBC's survey on their *Heaven and Earth* show, very few people think these are sins at all. Only nine per cent said they had been guilty of committing any of those sins. They must be saints. Of those who admitted giving in to one of the deadly sins, 79 per cent gave way to anger. Followed by pride, envy, lust, sloth and only 54 per cent admitted to the sin of greed.

Not unexpectedly, lust was the sin that both men and women said they would enjoy most. Surprisingly gluttony was a popular sin with women, but not with men.

But according to the same survey, attitudes towards sin have changed. Now we're more concerned with actions which hurt other people, rather than the seven deadly sins.

The new list of sins according to the people asked in this survey are:

1. Cruelty
2. Hypocrisy
3. Selfishness
4. Greed
5. Dishonesty
6. Bigotry
7. Adultery

You notice that greed is on both the old and new lists. In fact it could be argued that the new list is really the same list with a different emphasis.

By any standards there's a close connection between lust and adultery. And there's a strong case to be made that the basis of all sin is selfishness. What I'm delighted about is that people still think sin exists.

I wonder what your list would be? And before you start writing them, remember that as soon as you point a finger at anybody else, three fingers point back at yourself.

Personal Memo

To: YOU
Date: TODAY
From: THE BOSS
Subject: YOURSELF
Reference: LIFE

I AM God. Today I will be handling all of your problems. Please remember that I do need your help too.

If life happens to deliver a situation to you that you cannot handle, do not attempt to resolve it. Kindly put it in the SFGTD (something for God to do) box. All situations will be resolved, but in my time, not yours. Once the matter is placed into the box, do not hold onto it by worrying about it. Instead, focus on all the wonderful things that are present in your life now.

If you find yourself stuck in traffic, don't despair. There are people in this world for whom driving is an unheard-of privilege.

Should you have a bad day at work, think of the man who has been out of work for years.

Should you despair over a relationship gone bad, think of the person who has never known what it's like to love and be loved in return.

Should you grieve the passing of another weekend,
Think of the woman in dire straits, working twelve hours a day, seven days a week to feed her children.

Should your car break down, leaving you miles away from assistance, think of the paraplegic who would love the opportunity to take that walk.

Should you notice a new grey hair in the mirror, Think of the cancer patient in chemo who wishes she had hair to examine.

Should you find yourself at a loss and pondering what is life all about, asking what is my purpose? Be thankful! There are those who didn't live long enough to get the opportunity.

Should you find yourself the victim of other people's bitterness, ignorance, smallness or insecurities, remember, things could be worse! You could be one of them!

Should you decide to send this to a friend, thank you! You may have touched their life in ways you will never know.

Counting The Cost of The Demon Drink

It takes guts to tell someone you love them and mean it.

It takes even more guts to tell someone you hate them and mean it. Especially when that someone is your father.

And the young person who wrote the following letter has every reason to say it without guilt. Many a teenager will recognise the feeling as they wait for the drunken rows this weekend.

'My father was an alcoholic. I say *was* because he's dead now. Before he became ill I hadn't seen him for years. My mother and father had separated when I was a child.

'My father was an abusive alcoholic and as a child I couldn't understand the constant arguing and fighting. The fear of hearing a key in the lock in the early hours of the morning and the drunken chaos he would cause, still haunts me.

'As a child and more so as a teenager, I felt different – I didn't have a father. I was embarrassed if people talked about alcoholics. There was a stigma attached to being an alcoholic. I was ashamed of my father staggering down the street and I once denied that I knew him.

'I resented him, sometimes I even felt that I hated him. It was his fault that we weren't a proper family. My mother saw to it that we never wanted for anything but there will always be a gap where my father should have been.

'When my father first became ill, my mother insisted that we should go and visit him in hospital. I didn't want to go. Why should I? He had never bothered to be with us. Once I got rid of these feelings, and it took a lot of help from many friends, I did go to see him.

'He didn't admit that he was an alcoholic until a couple of weeks before he died. He confided to a friend that drink had taken everything he had: his wife, his family, his house, his sight, the power of his legs, the power of his arms, his speech and it would take his life. He was powerless to stop it.

'My father had to be spoon-fed. He got drink fed to him in a child's cup with a lid and was being lifted in and out of a wheelchair. It must have been so humiliating for him. His death was a painful experience, especially for my mother, as she still loved him. It's difficult to describe how I felt at the time of his death. It was sad because I had never really known him.

'Only when we sat up with him for the last few weeks did I really talk to him. Sometimes I would get a reaction, sometimes, not, but I talked anyway. I told him how I resented him and denied knowing him. I asked him to forgive me and I told him that I forgave him.

'When he died, it was a peaceful death and he had all his family and brothers and sisters with him. I felt more reconciled with him. I was happy that maybe we'd reached an understanding.

'I'm writing this not for sympathy or notice. But maybe someone reading it will identify with it and understand the damage alcoholism does.'

The Taters Family

- Some people never seem motivated to participate, but are just content to watch while others do the work. They are called Speck Taters.
- Some people never do anything to help, but are gifted at finding fault with the way others do the work. They are called Comment Taters.
- Some people are very bossy and like to tell others what to do but don't want to soil their own hands. They are called Dick Taters.
- Some people are always looking to cause problems by asking others to agree with them. It is too hot or too cold, too sour or too sweet. They are called Agie Taters.
- There are those who say they will help, but somehow just never get around to actually doing anything. They are called Hezzie Taters.
- Some people can put up a front and pretend to be someone they are not. They are called Emma Taters.
- Then there are those who love others and do what they say they will. They are always prepared to stop whatever they are doing and lend a helping hand. They bring real sunshine into the lives of others. They are called Sweet Taters.

Condom Contradictions

If your husband were HIV positive, would you use a condom to save your life? That is the dilemma facing the church in Africa today.

There is no doubt about it; the churches in southern Africa are on the front line battle against AIDS. It is causing church leaders on the ground to re-think traditional practices and to question the wisdom of edicts from Rome.

For a lifetime now, the defence of *Humanae Vitae*, the encyclical which banned artificial birth control, has been the criterion of loyalty for Rome. A priest could rape children and continue in good standing. But if he suggested that we should at least discuss the use of condoms to prevent the spread of AIDS, he'd get his walking papers.

Seventy per cent of the world's AIDS victims live, and sadly die, in southern Africa. A truly incredible 4.7 million people in South Africa itself have been infected with HIV. Each day 1,500 new cases occur. It is estimated they will have at least one million orphans as a result of AIDS related deaths within less than three years. Many of them will also be HIV positive.

It was that set of stark facts which prompted Bishop Kevin Dowling, the Bishop of Rustenburg on the borders of South Africa and Botswana, to say: 'The body of Christ has AIDS. I am with people dying every day. They are our people and there is no difference between the Church and AIDS sufferers. It is our people who are living and dying from this virus.'

He has been asking publicly if the hard-line stance against the use of condoms to help prevent the spread of the virus is justified. He said that the use of condoms is not wrong and they could be used when the purpose is to prevent death, rather than to prevent life. The difference in intention is obvious. He appealed to the well established principle of the lesser of two evils – when the choice is between two evils, we should choose the lesser evil.

Bishop Dowling knows that condoms are not the ultimate answer. They will not halt the spread of AIDS on their own. The surest way is to encourage responsible sex and to promote monogamous relationships.

But both are contrary to most African culture.

Dowling asks: 'What happens if a couple has three or four children, and one of the partners, for whatever reason, becomes HIV-positive? You've got young children, a marriage, and a sexual relationship which builds up that marriage. Do we say to that couple that for the rest of their lives they have to abstain from sex in order to avoid becoming infected?'

As Bishop Dowling put it: 'We have to decide whether we in the Church are part of the solution or part of the problem.'

The Garden of Life

Plant Three Rows Of Peas

1. Peace of mind
2. Peace of heart
3. Peace of soul

Plant Four Rows Of Squash

1. Squash gossip
2. Squash indifference
3. Squash grumbling
4. Squash selfishness

Plant Four Rows Of Lettuce

1. Lettucc be faithful
2. Lettuce be kind
3. Lettuce be patient
4. Lettuce really love one another

No Garden Is Without Turnips

1. Turnip for meetings
2. Turnip for service
3. Turnip to help one another

Every Garden Needs Thyme

1. Thyme for each other
2. Thyme for family
3. Thyme for friends

Water freely with patience and cultivate with love.

Suicide: The Pain, The Anger and The Sorrow

Suicide. Even the word has a sinister ring to it. It sends a shiver down the spine. So many people are struggling to cope with the death by suicide of a loved one.

An article I wrote about suicide prompted an anguished flood of letters. Let me try to outline some of that anguish.

After a suicide it is impossible to trust ever again. Spouses and parents all agree on that.

When somebody close to you takes their own life you recognise that you never really knew them. And if you didn't know your husband or your wife, after years of marriage, then could you ever know anyone? That's why the biggest casualty of a suicide is trust. You don't want to make yourself vulnerable again and no matter how well you think you know those close to you, you can never be sure. That's not just perplexing, it's truly devastating.

Many people admit they find it almost impossible to get their life back together again. It's like a jigsaw with the vital parts missing. No matter how your life evolves, there is always an unsolved mystery. The picture is never fully complete.

Then there's the guilt. One woman put it graphically when she described how, night after night, she talked to her husband about the pressures he was enduring at work.

Night after night she pleaded with him to allow her to help him, or to get help. Each time he assured her he could cope. When she found him dead in the car, guilt and anger consumed her.

For others the vital question was: 'Why was I not good enough for you?'

Then there were the usual questions. Why did you do it? Why did I not see it? How could I have prevented it?

Some found peace when they recognised that the only one who could answer those questions, is no longer around to be confronted. So the questions are futile.

For others their anger was directed at those who put pressure on them.

Work, financial institutions, doctors who didn't spot the depression. Surprisingly, few expressed their anger at those who took their own life. Yet when family members are left to face the crises of life alone, they begin to resent those who took the early exit from life.

Common to almost all the letters was a feeling of helplessness. Others make judgements about your life. The authorities have the right to ask questions, and in some cases invade your life to find answers that satisfy them. Occasionally people's homes were searched. They had no right to object to the mutilation of a post-mortem examination. People continue to make judgements about you and your family and you have no control over it. That leads to a sense of hopelessness and powerlessness.

Family members grieve differently. It depends on the relationship they had with the one who took their life. A husband or wife grieves differently to a son or a daughter. There is also the highly sensitive area of the two sides of the family. The family of the one who lives can often be at odds with the family members of the one who died. Sides are taken – his and hers. Almost every single one of the writers felt that 'If it hadn't been for you, this wouldn't have happened,' was sometimes said and more often implied.

One young person with great personal insight, said that her emotions are frozen in time. She was 11 when her father committed suicide and even though she is now in her early 20's she sometimes finds herself thinking, talking and laughing as if she were still an 11-year-old.

All of the letters wanted to make two points. Firstly, depression is an illness and can come on anyone suddenly. Without treatment it is uncontrollable. So suicide is not always or perhaps ever a selfish or cowardly act.

Secondly, with time, and with good grief, you will learn to look at that person's life with love and respect, and not judge them solely by the manner of their death.

The Voice of a Clerical Sex Abuse Victim

It was a very disturbing letter. My correspondent wrote:

'I decided to write to you now that you arc under fire. First I heard a woman tearing strips off you on radio, then I went to Mass and the priest mentioned you by name.

'He said you were a disgrace, always looking for notice; that you make life difficult for other priests by "spilling the beans" and you give ammunition to "those other churches". Everyone was furious with him, but as usual said nothing because he's the only priest we have.

'However, when I came home, and read your article, I saw exactly what you meant and I want to share some of my story with you. I am a single girl, in my 30s and am interested in my faith. I try to help out in my locality, usually in the parish set-up because really it's the only show in town.

'I realise mine is not the usual abuse case, but to me it's real, it's awful and it's ruining my life. We used to have a curate in our parish. He was a good enough man, more approachable than the parish priest, but clearly unhealthy, especially emotionally.

'He was overweight, always talking about his mother and would disappear for days during the week. His sermons were childish – "you're in a hurry today, so I won't keep you" sort of thing.

'At weddings, it was embarrassing because many of his references were double meaning. He was obviously an overgrown child, but still better than our other priest who is power mad, always looking for money and always giving out. If you cross him he gets you back at funerals and weddings by making things extremely awkward. So the curate seemed okay.

'Because of my job, I was able to buy a house just outside the district. The curate, by no means a man in the first flush of youth, started visiting me late at night. At first I thought he was lonely and I made him tea. But I felt demeaned even then by the vulgar way he used to look me up and down – something I now notice a lot of priests do.

'I couldn't wait to get him out of the house. After about three visits, he grabbed me one night as he was leaving.

'He forced me against the door and began opening his pants. I got sick with fear and screamed. But he put his hand over my mouth and pushed me into the bedroom. He lay on top of me and worst of all, he said nothing but his eyes were bulging and the smell off his breath made me sick.

'I kicked him as hard as I could, I screamed but he still molested me with his hands. I pleaded with him not to harm me and the only words he spoke were: "If you say anything about this I will make sure you lose your job."

'I don't know where I got the strength, but I bit his hand so hard it bled and he got off the bed, tidied himself and shrugged his shoulders. I will never know how I got through that night. I was off sick for many weeks, but could tell no one the reason.

'Eventually, I got the courage to tell the parish priest. After two or three minutes, he got up and started walking round and round. Then he put his hands over his ears and told me he didn't want to hear "this nonsense".

'That made me worse. He didn't believe me. Next day, he phoned me and said curtly he would seek help from the bishop. And from that day to this – about three years – I have never heard a word from anyone. The curate went off on what he called a sabbatical, got loads of presents from the parish and was given another appointment a year later.

'I am now so angry. A chance of promotion came up early this year and I applied. When I went for a reference, the parish priest said he couldn't give me one on account of "the incident". I realise now what you meant when you said the system was rotten to the core.

'Please do mention it in your column to let him know I haven't forgotten, and to remind people not to trust a parish priest or a Bishop to investigate their own.'

My advice was simple.

Thank you for your letter, I wish I could publish more to let readers know all you have endured, but I understand your position.

My immediate advice is for you to go to a recognised counsellor as soon as possible. Furthermore, you should report the incident to the police, preferably with the help of your counsellor. What you've endured was, at the very least, attempted rape and it is not acceptable that you should be denied justice or that such a person should still be in the ministry.

It is a disgrace that you were treated so deplorably by the priests and bishop.

The Catholic Church is entitled to conduct its own enquiry, but the state has a duty to investigate all crime – clerical or otherwise – without fear or favour.

The Dust Poem

Dust if you must, but wouldn't it be better
To paint a picture or write a letter,
Bake a cake or plant a seed,
Ponder the difference between want and need.

Dust if you must but there's not much time,
With rivers to swim and mountains to climb,
Music to hear and books to be read,
Friends to cherish and life to lead.

Dust if you must but the world's out there
With the sun in your eyes, the wind in your hair
A flutter of snow, a shower of rain,
This day will not come around again.

Dust if you must but bear in mind
Old age will come and it's not kind.
And when you go – as you must
You, yourself, will make more dust!

What Hope For The Men-Only Club?

Irish women feel betrayed by the Catholic Church and here's why.

When God became man, He chose a woman to be His mother. A woman brought Him into the world, women stood by Him as he left this world and a woman rushed to hug Him when He rose again. Two thousand years later women are relegated to second class citizenship and told they can serve in any capacity, except in Holy Orders at the altar, by the men who run the same Church which Jesus founded.

Is it any wonder women feel betrayed by the Catholic Church?

Hardly a day goes by that I don't receive letters from wonderfully articulate, marvellously dedicated but extremely angry women. They argue with clarity and cogency that they are being patronised by this Men Only Club.

They seethe when they are arrogantly squelched by heavy-handed authoritarianism.

That's what annoys so many of the women who contact me. They are still treated as if their role is to 'help priests to run the Church better.'

One woman put it graphically: 'My parish priest told me that I could serve God by cleaning the Church, arranging the flowers, making tea for the bishop at confirmation and occasionally by reading and giving out Communion at Mass.' It's the pray, pay and obey system of abuse all over again. Women now realise that they will never be allowed to serve as priests as long as the men only club can do without them. They know that any kind of man will be preferred to them. It's not a question of ability, but virility.

It has finally dawned on most intelligent women that they will not become priests, because men have power. They will not be allowed to crack the all male power base which the priesthood is at present. For most women now, it is no longer a question of good public relations. It is a question of justice – plain and simple.

It is, women say, indefensible that the all – male priesthood should have the only say on this matter. Not only that but their arguments are so weak that they have closed discussion on the issue, said it can't even be talked about.

How could anyone with a reasonable argument to make not engage in respectful dialogue?

To dismiss half the population of the world as being unworthy and unable to serve God and their community as priest, is unwise, unhealthy and unjust.

Put simply, it is a scandal and probably one of the main reasons why God sends so few vocations to the church in the Western World.

There is still a good supply of vocations to the male priesthood in poorer countries where women are treated as inferiors. That's no coincidence.

There are those in authority who say that the Catholic Church CAN'T ordain women because Jesus chose an all-male priesthood and because tradition says there has never been women priests.

But the majority of theologians (many of whom are now women) and scripture scholars say their arguments don't hold water.

First of all, the scriptures reflect the times in which they were written. (Slavery is justified in the Old and New Testaments. Does that mean we should never have fought for its abolition?)

Women in those times were second-class citizens and it would have been inconceivable for them to be in positions of leadership in such a society. Jesus went out of his way to proclaim the dignity of women even when it scandalised the religious leaders of His time.

We live in different times now and, women argue, if Jesus were alive today He would be the first to give them their proper place in the Church.

He would not condemn them to the slavery of second-class citizenship. He would welcome their giftedness and would use their unique qualities to spread His message of love and redemption to a world in such dire need of compassion.

Furthermore, Jesus made the Eucharist the central act of worship. Yet more and more of His people will be deprived of Mass because of a lack of priests while Church authorities continue to bar one half of the world's population from the priesthood.

Sadly, even the most dedicated are getting the message, now. You won't get into our club, not now, not ever. In short, you might well save our Church, but we'd prefer to hold our power. That's what I hear the still-interested women say and it saddens me.

But one must always live in hope. We are a risen people. New life will come despite the deadwood.

The Value of Time

To realise
the value of one hour:
Ask the lovers who are waiting to meet.

To realise
the value of one minute:
Ask a person
Who has missed the train, bus, or plane.

To realise
the value of one second:
Ask a person
Who has survived an accident.

To realise
the value of one millisecond:
Ask the person who has won a silver medal
In the Olympics.

Time waits for no one. Treasure every moment you have. You will
treasure it even more when you can share it
With someone special.

To realise the value of a friend:
Lose one.

How To Destroy a Life

'As I sit alone, the person that comes to mind is you and that is why I write this letter to you.

'I have worked for the past 20 years. I am married with children and have a lovely home but feel totally devastated at what has happened to me. I worked locally, was very well liked and loved my work.

'Then a girl joined the staff about a year ago who was pleasant and we all got along fine. We discovered she was having an affair with a married man we all knew and everyone was talking. Then out of the blue she left and this man come into work accusing me of spreading it around that he was having an affair with her.

'I didn't care much at the time as it was not my business, so I refused to let it bother me. About six weeks later this person came in and questioned me about it again. I told him what he did in his life was his problem not mine. But he roared at me. I need my head examined, I was a lunatic, a f.....g bitch and worse.

'I was horrified. I was so ill at the thought of someone doing this to another person and it didn't stop at that. He told my employer, who was a friend of his, that he should get rid of me.

'He was so awful to me, he so demeaned and downgraded me, that I had to leave. So I left. I did not tell anyone what happened and my husband and children had to take my mood swings and bad temper for the next two months until I could find work again. And I did.

'I got a job in an office all on my own away from everyone other than the boys I worked with. They were really nice and helpful.

'Then my new employer started giving me verbal abuse and I thought I'm never going down this road again. So one Friday when he came into the office and was rather abusive again I decided to quit.

"I know in my heart that from my other experiences I cannot cope with being shouted at and verbally abused. I have lost my confidence but most of all I have lost the will to go on. People have said forget about it. But it won't leave me. It is there and I will never get over it.

'I want you to ask employers why they have to be so abusive to staff? And why, in my first experience, did my employer take the word of his friend and never ask me? To explain why this man could come into my work, abuse me in such a way for something I'm not guilty of doing?

'If I do kill myself - and I feel now that is the only thing to do – will they live with this?

'I hope they listen and ask themselves: Why destroy a life? Why make people sad? Why make people lonely? We only have one life and I see no solution ahead. Please don't let this happen to anyone else.'

When I'm An Old Lady

When I'm an old lady, I'll play with each kid,
And bring so much happiness… just as they did.
I want to pay back all the joy they've provided,
Returning each deed, Oh, they'll be so excited!
When I'm an old lady and live with my kids!

I'll write on the wall with reds, whites and blues,
And bounce on the furniture wearing my shoes.
I'll drink from the carton and then leave it out.
I'll stuff all the toilets and oh, how they'll shout!
When I'm an old lady and live with my kids!

When they're on the phone and just out of reach,
I'll get into things like sugar and bleach,
Oh, they'll snap their fingers and then shake their head,
And when that is done I'll hide under the bed!
When I'm an old lady and live with my kids!

And later in bed, I'll lay back and sigh,
I'll thank God in Prayer and then close my eyes.
My kids will look down with a smile slowly creeping,
And say with a groan. "She's so sweet, when she's sleeping!"
When I'm an old lady and live with my kids.

Beating The Bullies

Bullying is a major problem in Irish schools, homes and the workplace. That's the conclusion I've come to as a result of the letters the I've got over the last 30 years; it is also, in my opinion, the root cause of many suicides in our country.

Because of the nature of suicide, it's hard to prove a direct link with bullying. However, the results of bullying are fear, anger, sadness, humiliation, and dismantling of self-belief. Those are the circumstances that will drive a person to think of suicide.

In modern Ireland bullying is almost institutionalised. In our efforts to be top of the league of greed, we are willing to sell our soul. If this means bullying our way to the top, then so be it.

Look at the image we use for our prosperity. The Celtic Tiger. There is nothing friendly, or attractive, about a tiger. Celtic or otherwise. It is ferociously powerful, dangerous and inspires fear – a classic definition of bullying.

Experts tell us that bullies intimidate others mentally, physically and emotionally. It means putting others in uncomfortable situations, personal intimidation and in hurting the weak. You can see it in physical aggression, extortion, abusive behaviour, deliberately excluding others, slagging them off, name calling, hitting people, making cutting remarks, spreading rumours, true or false, about others. They are all bullying and hurtful in their own way.

Bullying is wrong because it takes away the basic human right each of us has to be who and what God made us.

As in all kinds of emotional disorder, secrecy is the enemy of healthy living. There is nothing wrong in asking for help.

It's wrong though to retaliate. Don't hit back physically because you could be rightly accused of bullying yourself.

Keep everything in perspective. Tell the truth and don't exaggerate. Work at developing your own friendships.

Don't allow yourself to become isolated. Do talk to adults you can trust. These are just a few helpful suggestions made in a book called *Bullying In The Work-Place, Home and School* by Tony Byrne, Kathleen Maguire and Brendan Byrne.

Taking Care of The Carers

More and more families are being asked to care for their elderly.

It is GOOD that people live longer. Yet, it demands great sacrifices if they are cared for at home. It's hard to allow them the independence they deserve with the care they need.

Too often caring is left to an individual. Governments are pathetic in recognising the selfless dedication of carers.

I got a super letter from a carer recently who looks after his ailing wife. First, he wanted me to point out that carers can be male. And they too suffer from burnout.

'As somebody who has been through the mill, let me warn your readers about the signs of burnout and once it is recognised, suggest a few tips to prevent it in the future', he wrote.

'For me, it started with permanent exhaustion. When I went to bed I couldn't sleep. The real warning came when I found myself crying practically every day for no reason.

'I was irritable with the children and couldn't control my temper, even with my wife who was supposed to be the object of my care and affection.'

It was his doctor who recognised the signs and, between them, they worked out a programme of care for both him and his wife.

'Now I make sure to look after my own health. I try to get enough rest and exercise on the principle that, if I don't look after myself, I am not going to be much help to my wife.

'I go to my doctor once a month to make sure I don't have another breakdown.

'I've struggled to have a normal life. I build little treats into the day. Those respites are as important as getting up in the middle of the night to look after my wife who is completely incapable of doing anything for herself.

'I choose between what is important and what's not. The important I try to do and the unimportant I simply dismiss.

'The first thing I had to accept was that my wife's illness was not my fault. There is nothing I can do about it and there is nothing I can do to stop it. All I can do is care for her.

'No matter what the demands made upon me by her relatives, professionals who visited the house, and frequently my wife herself, I accepted that I was only human and didn't feel guilty when I couldn't do the impossible.

'My wife didn't want to let others see how helpless she was. For a while I fell into the trap and tried to do it all alone. I don't anymore. If she is to get the proper care, then I need help too.

'At least twice a year I try to get a complete break. I owe it to myself, but more importantly I owe my wife the break too. She goes to respite care and finds the break away from the house does her good.

'I just do normal things for a week or ten days and come back refreshed.

'In the beginning I used to promise my wife that I would never put her in long term care. I don't anymore.

'I'll try my best to keep her at home for as long as she is comfortable. However, if I thought long-term care was better for her than the care I am giving her, I would make sure she got it.

'I know she doesn't particularly like it but, I have to be honest, there may come a time when she will be better looked after in a different environment.

'As regards those who come to visit me, I don't have many requests. But I would mention these few.

'Don't give me unsolicited advice – I'd prefer to hear words of encouragement.

'Practical support is best of all. Bring a cake or a ready-made lunch or a little treat. Flowers are O.K. occasionally, but you can't eat them'.

That's what the man said in his letter to me so I thought I would pass it onto you, because it seemed such a practical, no nonsense, realistic approach.

Be With Us, Lord...

In January, the month of darkness and frost. Be with us, Lord.

In February, the month of rain, wind and snow. Be with us, Lord.

In March, the month of farmers, lambs and new life. Be with us, Lord.

In April, the month of swallows, growth and green grass. Be with us, Lord.

In May, the month of the cuckoo, the flowers and summer. Be with us, Lord.

In June, the month of examinations, the mid-summer and sun. Be with us, Lord.

In July, the month of holidays, the dry grass and summer's end. Be with us, Lord.

In August, the month of harvest, wheat and corn. Be with us, Lord.

In September, the month of fruits and schools. Be with us, Lord.

In October, the month of falling leaves, nuts and Halloween. Be with us, Lord.

In November, the month of darkness, and emptiness. Be with us, Lord.

In December, the month of the gift, the light and Our Saviour. Be with us, Lord.

We ask you, Lord, for your strength as we commit ourselves to work for:

Respect for the earth, peace for its people, Love in our lives, Delight in the good, forgiveness for past wrongs, And from now on a new start. We ask this blessing in God's name. Amen.

(Contributed by a Reader)